I0690670

THE MAN OF A THOUSAND FACES

Volume Six

AIRSHIP 27 PRODUCTIONS

SECRET AGENT X: VOLUME SIX
An Airship 27 Production

"Island in the Sky" © 2018 Fred Adams Jr.
"Escape from Zakopane" © 2018 Kaushik Karforma
"Dead do Dance" © 2018 Fred Schildiner

Cover and interior illustrations © 2018 Rob Davis

Managing Editor: Ron Fortier
Associate Editor: Jonathan Sweet
Production and design by Rob Davis
Marketing and Promotions Manager: Michael Vance

Published by Airship 27 Productions
airship27hangar.com

ISBN: 978-1-946183-32-3
(ISBN-10: 1-946183-32-6)

Printed in the United States of America

10 9 8 7 6 5 4 3 2 1

SECRET AGENT "X" ANTHOLOGY
Volume Six
Table of Contents

SECRET AGENT "X"

Island in the Sky

by Fred Adams Jr.

Midnight. The moon shone white on the Arctic ice cap as the hangar door opened and a man named Bakewell clad in a fur-collared parka stepped out. He turned, and the pale moon was doubled in the eye pieces of a full head mask that made him look like an anteater with a ribbed proboscis ending in a square pouch.

He glanced at the wind sock; dead calm for the first time in hours. Time to light the flares. Bakewell waved to Shaklee inside the shed to get on the radio and signal the ship. He pulled the first of the fusee from a canvas sack hanging at his hip and twisted the striker from the body of the flare. He scraped the end of the fusee with the abrasive striker, and a red flame shot from the tip. He rammed the spike at the fusee's other end into the ice and counted fifty paces before lighting another. In five minutes, a glowing rectangle painted the ice cap a bright red around the steel ribbed mooring tower that stood a full eighty feet tall.

Time to wait. He didn't have to wait long. The droning of motors rumbled in the distance. Coming from the South, he thought, then snorted. Up here, everything comes from the South. Before he saw the airship, Bakewell saw its shadow, black, enormous, crawling across the ice. No matter how many times he saw Delos, its sheer size amazed him. The dirigible was as big as five or six football fields and required a clear space to moor afforded only by areas of desert—or a polar ice cap, although he had heard the ship had an inflatable base to allow it to land on water.

But Delos was not going to land, exactly. It had not touched ground since it first took off more than a year before. Tethered to the mooring mast, the ship would still be thirty feet off the ground, secured by the mast and cables hooked to the ice. As the ship floated into position, precisely guided by the manipulation of its twelve propellers by the pilot, the moon disappeared, and the black velvet shadow covered the base like a shroud.

Bakewell opened a steel panel at the base of the mooring mast and turned a large two-handed wheel. Eighty feet in the air, a coupler like a steel pincer rotated into position and opened with a dull clank.

More men came from the shed, dressed like Bakewell. Steel hooks snaked from the three-story gondola of the ship, more like a floating warehouse than a passenger compartment. The masked men secured the lines, making the dirigible safe from the unpredictable polar winds, and stepped back as a ramp lowered from the bottom of the gondola. Floodlights came on around the ramp, and four tanker trucks rumbled across the ice from the hangar to stop below the dirigible.

An umbilicus dropped from the rear of the ship. A moment to connect, and fuel was soon gurgling from each truck in its turn into the Delos' tanks.

The ramp contained an escalator-like conveyor, and with the whine of an electric motor and a ratcheting of gears, it began scrolling upward, taking dozens of crates into the gondola as the team loaded them onto the belt. Stenciled on the sides of the crates were words: beef, salmon, rice, champagne, and one heavy iron-bound box marked munitions.

The loading was efficient, and in less than a half hour, the ramp was raised, the tethering cables withdrawn, and inside the shed, Shaklee heard two words from Delos' pilot crackle over the wireless: Cast off.

Shaklee waved to Bakewell, who strode to the base of the mooring tower and pulled down on a heavy red lever. Overhead, the coupler that held Delos to the mooring tower opened, and the Delos began to drift away. Once clear of the coupler, the pilot engaged the multiple propellers and the ship gently glided away from the tower.

It would be a full minute before Bakewell saw the moon again.

X X X

Robert Haines hung up the phone. He stared at the slick residue on the black handset where his hand had touched it. Every solid object felt like a Hershey bar in hot weather. First stage of The Virus. He crossed the thick green carpet of his office in the towering skyscraper that he owned. The building housed the corporate offices of Consolidated Firearms, the industrial company that he'd built from scratch. From the window he saw the ant-like people on 46th Street below. Not ants, he thought with a snort, cockroaches. The first signs of society unraveling had appeared. Mobs and looters. The police were trying to maintain order, but it was quickly slipping away.

What was it Yeats wrote, he thought, "Things fall apart; the centre cannot hold." The European nations were handling the whole business more stoically, but they'd suffered a plague before. America had suffered the Spanish Influenza epidemic twenty years before, and the cholera epidemic in the last century, but nothing on the scale of the Black Plague of the Middle Ages, and nothing so devastating as this.

The Mystery Virus, as the press called it, had begun in Africa, its root in the Belgian Congo, where every attempt was made to isolate it to the point of imposing quarantine on the whole country, but the infected slipped through, and the plague spread across Africa and into Asia and Europe. Then it found its way to the Western Hemisphere, despite all attempts to keep immigrants and imports out. You can't quarantine the air, Haines thought, like Canute ordering the waves to cease.

The Mystery Virus, known now as simply The Virus, as if there had never been another, attacked the cell walls of humans and some higher primates, monkeys, gibbons, gorillas. The cell walls deteriorated, and to paraphrase Yeats, cells fall apart. The skin went first, exposed to the air, leading to the constant slimy residue on hair, clothing, and everything one touched. In advanced stages, the skin would come off in small bits then larger ones. Wipe your face one morning, and it might come off in your hand like a Halloween mask. Blindness set in as The Virus attacked the surface of the eyes.

But by then, The Virus, entering the body through the lungs would have begun breaking down internal organs. The worst aspect of The Virus was its pace. Death crept cruelly slow, months of increasing agony before the heart mercifully stopped. Many had opted for a gun or poison or simply throwing themselves out a window or off a bridge.

Then some scientist working feverishly in a lab somewhere discovered that The Virus weakened with a decrease in air pressure; it dissipated at altitudes approaching fourteen thousand feet, and recovery, albeit temporary, was possible. Probably give him a Nobel Prize, thought Haines, if he survives to accept it, and if there's anyone left to hand it to him.

Then the mass migration had begun toward the mountains; Mount McKinley where a temporary White House was in operation, Saint Elias, Foraker, by people desperate to save themselves and their families. But the mountains could hold only so many and no more.

He crossed to the small bathroom at the other end of his office. Haines splashed cold water on his face and looked into the mirror and saw his forty-seven years accelerated by ten. He still had a full head of iron grey hair and a thick moustache to match under a broad nose. Water dripped from his cleft chin, and he reached for a towel to carefully blot his face, lest he wipe away a layer of skin with it.

The message he'd received two days before gave him hope, a way to survive the crisis. It seemed too good to be true, but Haines refused to think that way, because in his experience, things that seem too good to be true usually are, and he wanted so much to believe.

X X X

Broadway was dark.

The hundreds of thousands of chase lights, neon tubes and colored bulbs that lit the marquees of the dozens of theaters of the Great White Way were idle. The klieg lights that crisscrossed the sky for the premiere of a new musical were replaced by the spotlights of the police patrol cars enforcing New York City's sundown curfew.

Agent X rode in the back seat of one of those cars as it prowled the Manhattan pavement. The officers in the front seat didn't know who X was or why he was on the benighted streets, only where he was going.

The patrol car passed Big Apple corner at 54th and slowed as the white cone of the spotlight caught a knot of men in front of a deli, some standing on the sidewalk as others inside threw baskets of food through the smashed window.

"Should we stop?" said the driver.

"Can't," his partner replied. "We have to deliver our bearded friend back there." He jerked his thumb toward the back seat. "Orders. I'd call it in, but by the time another car gets here, they'll be gone."

"Friend," an ironic choice of words, X thought. If they knew who I really am, they wouldn't take me to the Royal Court, they'd take me downtown and book me.

Though he fought on the side of law and order, Agent X's covert operations and secret identities were regarded by the police as "a subversive interference" and he was regarded as an outlaw in most circles. But he consistently delivered some of the most dangerous criminals in the world to an often ungrateful establishment. A friend indeed.

The officers left X on the sidewalk in front of the Royal Court Theater. Its marquee too was dark, as all the others had been for the last two weeks on Broadway because the streets were too dangerous at night, and were becoming equally dangerous in the daytime. The theaters were closed at night as were most of the shops and businesses in New York and every other city in the United States and the world in general.

X passed the ticket booth and counted the brass doors to the foyer from left to right. He pulled the handle of the third door and it swung open. As soon as he stepped into the lobby, it would be locked again. X passed the darkened candy counter and opened the swinging door into the auditorium.

On the stage, a single bare bulb burned in a shadeless floor lamp, the ghost light common to most empty theaters. There are far worse things to fear than ghosts, X thought as he followed the aisle to a short flight of steps beside the orchestra pit. He climbed the six steps and crossed the empty stage. His feet echoed in the empty auditorium as he crossed from stage right to stage left, his shadow cast by the ghost light following him against the featureless scrim at the back wall.

Some actors play their roles for money and applause, he thought. Shakespeare was right; all the world is a stage, but I play my roles for the sake of the nation, and no one ever applauds.

Past the wings, X saw a light shining from an open dressing room door. He rapped on the frame with his knuckles and stepped inside. The vanity lights were lit over the makeup mirrors, but the chairs were all empty. One had been pulled to the center of the room and a small table stood before it. The table was empty except for a thick brown button-and-string envelope.

He looked at himself in one of the lighted mirrors. He had come to dislike them because more times than not, when he looked into a mirror, he rarely saw the face he recognized as his own. Tonight, a bearded man with a touch of grey along the jaw line peered back at him through thick gold-rimmed spectacles perched on a blunt nose.

"Welcome, Agent X." The voice of the mysterious K-9, the man who assigned and directed X's operations, rasped through an electronic filter. X heard a shuffling sound behind an ornate dressing screen in a far corner of the room. He had never seen K-9's face, and tonight would be no exception.

"Please sit down and open the envelope."

X sat in the chair, undid the string, and dumped the contents of the envelope onto the table. Along with the customary file folders and photographs, he saw an unusual object.

"For what it's worth, that is how the epidemic began," K-9's voice grated.

Agent X lifted the Congolese bank note sealed between two small panes of glass. "I don't see—"

"Look under the second digit of the serial number."

X strained his eyes and held the note closer to the light. Almost invisible, a brown dot the size of a pinpoint lay under the line of numerals. "What better way to spread a disease," he said. "Everyone handles money all day long, especially a small denomination bill like this one, and no one thinks twice about it."

"And as it was handled, the coating that encased The Virus wore away and released it. There is no doubt," said K-9 from behind the screen. "This epidemic was intentional and premeditated."

X set the evidence on the table in front of him, frowning at the slick residue his fingers left on the glass. "Plague-sweat," the newspapers called it. "But why would anyone launch a plague that will ultimately destroy everyone, himself included?"

"Normally, we would begin with that question, motive leading to perpetrator, but in this case, we have to work in reverse. Who has the means to create such a disease and the means to spread it?"

"A plot like this could cost hundreds of millions of dollars. Surely no government would do such a thing."

"Agreed," said K-9. "Which leaves us to look in the private sector. Only three pharmaceutical companies exist that have the technical capability to create something like The Virus, and all three are American: Century Biochemical Corporation, Capstone Pharmaceutical, and Montrose Research."

"And all three are working around the clock to find a cure."

"Of the three, Century is the largest, but Montrose Research is close behind, and its owner, Elias Montrose has been aggressive in his pursuit of the top spot for years. He has persistently hired away the best minds and the best researchers from Century and Capstone. He has the technical means, and he has the money."

"But ambition doesn't mean that he'd destroy the world to prove his company is the greatest."

"It is not ambition that concerns us, Agent X, it is obsession."

"To rule or ruin?"

"Possibly. Apart from that issue, there is the Delos. You've heard of it?"

"The super dirigible? Who hasn't?"

"Our intelligence reports show communication between Elias Montrose and the owners of the Wall Street Thirty, the thirty most powerful corporations on the New York Stock Exchange, cutting across all aspects of the economy from Industry to Finance, the giants of the world economy."

"You said 'communication;' of what nature?"

"Delos can fly over the fourteen-thousand foot level, safe from The Virus. He is offering them sanctuary."

"In exchange for what?"

"That is what you will find out. His motives may be pure, but his past suggests otherwise. He, thus far, is our only likely avenue of investigation. Open the packet in front of you. Your orders are effective immediately."

X opened the sealed pouch, and as he did, he heard a door close softly. K-9 had left the room, and he was, from that moment, on his own to save the world and to save himself along with it.

X X X

Back in his town house, X peeled the false beard from his jaw and wiped the spirit gum away with alcohol. The thick, flat nose came next, and then the special pancake makeup that gave his skin the ruddy look of an alcoholic.

In a moment, X gazed at his own features in the mirror. No matter how many times he changed his identity, he always felt a sense of relief to see his own face and be himself again, if only for a few moments. Lesser men might have been driven mad by such total immersion in another's identity. Years ago, X had suffered nightmares about peeling off one face after another and never finding his own under them, but years had passed without that awful dream.

He switched on the big RCA radio in the corner of his living room, and as he waited for it to warm up, he fixed himself a gin and tonic in the kitchen. Instead of its regular broadcast of a live big-band performance from the Roseland Ballroom, WOR was presenting a program of recorded music.

Benny Goodman's "One O'clock Jump" poured out of the speaker, and X sank into his easy chair. He put the cool glass against his forehead and closed his eyes. He knew he should be studying the packet of information K-9 had given him, but he needed just a few minutes to be himself before he prepared to become someone else once again.

He opened the file and drew out a sheaf of photographs. Another face, another set of mannerisms, another walk, another voice; Time to begin the elaborate task of becoming Robert Haines.

X X X

The next morning, X slid into the seat of a drugstore phone booth. He dialed a number he knew from memory and waited as the phone rang three times at the other end of the line before a voice said, "*New York Herald*. How may I direct your call?"

"May I please speak with Betty Dale." X said.

"One moment, sir. I'll connect you." The phone clicked and buzzed in his ear, then a bright voice said, "City Desk; Betty Dale speaking."

"Miss Dale, you may not remember me. Some time ago, you assisted me in research for my doctoral dissertation on 20th Century American history. I wondered whether you might help me once again with some *ex*-tra information."

Betty drew in a long breath and her bright tone became serious. "Yes, sir, I remember you quite well. What material do you need?"

"I need information beyond the ordinary reporting on Elias Montrose, his company, and the Delos. I need deep information, not the usual gloss, whatever you can provide."

"Very well. Anything else?"

"Any information you can provide me about Robert Haines of Consolidated Firearms, particularly the past two to three years."

"And how soon do you need this information?"

"As soon as possible. Tomorrow noon at the latest."

"I'll see what I can do for you."

"Thank you. May I call you later?"

"Please do."

The line went dead. Betty Dale was the only person outside a few in the Agency that X served who knew his identity, and she understood all too well what the guarded conversation meant. It meant that X was about to embark on another perilous mission. On one hand, she hated to see her friend go into the field and risk his life once again, but on the other, she realized that the more she helped X, the better his chances were of coming back alive at the mission's end.

She was about to leave her desk for the morgue when Max Willis, a fellow reporter strolled by her desk. "See my piece in this morning's edition?" He took off his rimless spectacles and polished them on his shirt.

It took all of Betty's self-control to not roll her eyes. "Yes, Max, I saw it; another nice byline over the fold. I can hear the Pulitzer Prize committee climbing the stairs right now."

"Aw, come on, Betty," Max said, giving her a lopsided grin. "You aren't still sore because I scooped you on the City Council scandal last week."

Max had stolen the story right from under her, grabbed the headline and the byline, and gave her no credit at all.

"No, Max, I'm not sore. All's fair in love and journalism, right?" Her voice was tinged with sarcasm.

"Tell you what," Willis said, pushing his glasses up his nose for the third time since the conversation began. "Let me make it up to you. Let me buy you dinner tonight."

"Can't, Max," Betty said. "I have a lot of work to do if I'm going to keep up with the *Herald's* star reporter. Unlike you, I have no laurels to rest on."

"How about a rain check?"

"I hear there's a drought coming."

"Okay, okay," he said with a laugh, "but the offer stands." He walked away, hands in his pockets, whistling.

Betty ground her teeth. Max's cutthroat approach to the job was bad enough, but more than anything, she wished Max would take the hint and stop pestering her. There was only one man in her life, and right now, he needed her help.

X X X

X parked his car in an alley that afforded him a clear view of Robert Haines' building on 46th Street. If Haines behaved according to habit, he would arrive promptly at eight o'clock in the big black Packard sedan. A delivery van had been parked directly in front of the building to force Haines' driver to park up the block. X checked his watch. Any minute, the car would arrive.

He reached under the dashboard and retrieved a small movie camera, small at least in comparison to the bulky, heavy units Hollywood used. He gave the key a quick turn to ensure that the mechanism was wound, put the view finder to his eye to set the focus, and waited.

He didn't have to wait long. As the clock on the Mackenzie Building down the street tolled the hour, the Packard sedan turned the corner into 46th Street traffic. Finding no place to park in front of the building, the driver went nearly a block away to pull to the curb. He came around to open the passenger door, and Robert Haines climbed out of the back seat.

X tripped a lever, and the camera began to whir. He captured Robert Haines on film as he tucked a briefcase under his arm and set off down the sidewalk. X's interest was in two things, Haines' carriage and a slight limp that resulted from a broken ankle two years before. In a minute, Haines disappeared behind the delivery truck and into the building, but X had captured enough of Haines' mannerisms on film. With a little study and practice, he would convincingly pass himself off as the firearms manufacturer.

X X X

Betty Dale left her desk a few minutes after eleven with a thick envelope under her arm. She had located not only press clippings, but also interview transcripts and reporters' notes containing allegations from anonymous sources and the kind of gossip and dirt the *Tattler* might print, but that no respectable newspaper would publish.

As she walked down the hall toward the elevator, she saw the grinning

Max Willis coming the other way. "Hey, Betty, going to lunch? Can I tag along? I'll buy."

She shook her head and pointed across the hall to the door of the Ladies' room. "I'm not going to lunch. And no, you can't tag along."

Max's face fell as she crossed the hall to the rest room door. "Bye, Max." She waved as the door closed between them.

Betty huffed in frustration. The man was infuriating. She looked at her watch. She'd have to hurry to be on time as it was, and this delay made things worse. She waited two minutes and opened the door a crack to look down the hallway. Willis was nowhere in sight. She hurried to the elevator and pushed the Down button. In another minute, she was on the sidewalk hailing a cab to take her to Washington Square.

The cab followed Fifth Avenue to its end, and Betty arrived at the Arch a few minutes after twelve, cursing the traffic that made her late. The Square was bustling with people on their lunch hours, strolling in the warm spring sun. She scanned the benches around the square and saw a number of men sitting alone. Three of them were reading newspapers. Only one was wearing a Homburg.

She brushed a strand of honey blonde hair from her forehead and crossed the park to the bench. Then man in the hat looked up at her and tipped his head forward in greeting then went back to his newspaper. He wore half-framed glasses perched on a long nose over a small brush of a moustache.

Betty sat and laid the envelope between them. She opened her purse and took out a cigarette. "Excuse me, do you have light?"

The man in the Homburg smiled and pulled a silver cigarette lighter from his pocket. He flicked the wheel, and cupped his hand around the flame. As she leaned in to light her cigarette, Betty closed her fingers and thumb over the man's wrist and looked into his eyes. No matter how he might change his face, Betty always knew his eyes. She whispered, "I know you can't tell me where you're going or what you have to do, but please, come back to me."

Her cigarette lit, Betty stood and walked away, fighting tears.

X watched her pass through the arch and raise her arm to hail a taxi. He allowed himself a moment for maudlin reflection, then set sentiment aside and turned his focus back to the mission.

X X X

"Please, come back to me."

Robert Haines rifled the drawers of the Manhattan apartment he used when he worked in his corporate offices. He was selecting cold weather clothing. His instructions said one suitcase only; space was at a premium.

The executive's eyes strayed to a photograph of his late wife Myra, and he almost put it in his bag frame and all. She was three years gone, and thank God she didn't have to suffer The Virus. He looked at the wedding ring on his finger and after a moment's consideration, decided to leave it on. Haines didn't know what he would have done had she still been alive and he had to choose between survival alone and a slow painful death by her side.

He shook his head dismissing the thought. This is Year Zero. The past is a millstone. He pulled the dresser away from the wall and knelt to peel back a corner of the carpet. Below it was a key-lock safe. Haines fumbled with the key, his fingers slippery with the ever present plague-sweat.

In the safe he found banded stacks of money in mixed denominations. These, he pushed aside, realizing that money would soon be worthless. He had once scoffed at the words of a wild-eyed doom-saying preacher on a Madison Avenue street corner: "'They shall cast their silver into the streets.' Thus saith Ezekiel!"

Not silver, Haines thought, silver certificates. He reached under the money and drew out a small velvet sack. He opened the drawstring and poured a double dozen diamonds into his palm. These, he thought will never lose their value; vanity and adornment aside, they will always be useful for industrial purposes, and when this panic has passed, they will be more valuable than ever. First, he had to survive.

He thrust the diamonds into a trouser pocket and opened the top drawer of his desk. A compact .32 caliber automatic lay on top of his papers like a faithful friend. Haines had a hand in designing it himself, and it was one of his best-selling firearms. He checked the magazine. Full. Montrose promised security, but Haines still had to make it to the airfield across the river in Jersey.

A knock at the door. It was Simms, his driver. Time to leave. Haines opened the door and was startled to see himself in the doorway. "What the devil—?" His doppelganger raised a small revolver and pointed it at Haines' chest.

"Not a word." Agent X pushed Haines gently into the room and closed the door behind him, locking it. "You have an invitation to Delos," X said. "Hand it over."

"You think you'll pass yourself off as me and save your worthless hide from The Virus," Haines snarled. "The hell you will. I don't know how you found out, but I'll be damned if you're taking my place." Haines' hand shot forward, spearing X in the chest and throwing the agent off balance. Haines waded in and grappled with X for the pistol.

The businessman was stronger than he looked, and X had to use the Oriental arts to twist from the executive's grasp and throw him to the floor. The fall knocked the wind out of Haines, and X easily subdued him, cuffing his hands behind his back and stuffing a handkerchief into his mouth.

"You're about to become a hero, Mister Haines," X said. "You're going to save the world. All you have to do is sit still while I do all the work. Just tell me where the invitation is."

Haines shook his head, his eyes blazing fiercely. His grunt around the gag was distinctly negative. X shook his head. "I hate to do things this way, but—" He reached into his coat and pulled out a grey rubber bulb with a spray spout. He aimed it at Haines' nose and squeezed. A puff of grey powder burst from the nozzle, and in seconds, Haines' eyes rolled back in his head and he stopped struggling.

In the executive's trouser pockets, X found a pistol, a money clip, and a handful of change. In his vest, X found a pocket watch whose chain joined a gold double eagle with a .45 caliber slug lodged in it. X took the plain golden band from Haines' finger and slipped it on his own; a snug fit, but it got past the second knuckle with a little bit of urging. In his suit jacket, X found an envelope and a small blue velvet bag. The bag held diamonds, and the envelope held Haines' invitation from Montrose.

"Hunnicutt corporate hangar, Kensington Airfield, eight p.m." it read. Kensington Airfield was a private airstrip across the river in New Jersey. X looked at the clock. Seven-ten. Fifty minutes to make it on time.

Someone knocked, three fast-two slow-three fast. It was the pickup team. X opened the door and two men in coveralls with a trunk on a dolly stood in the hallway. He motioned them inside. One of them opened the trunk and took out a Gladstone bag. They quickly scooped up the lethargic Haines and closed him in the trunk. In a moment, they were gone.

X opened the bag and from beneath its false bottom, he retrieved a small metal case and went into the bathroom to check his disguise in the mirror. Plague-sweat made the durability of appliances and makeup chancy at best, and he was afraid that the tussle with Haines had loosened one of his appliances.

The false nose was slightly askew, but easily corrected. So far, the moustache and chin were intact. A little touch-up with makeup from his kit, and he looked more than convincing. X had seen the corporate car from Consolidated Firearms idling at the curb. He'd had to slip around to the rear entrance of the apartment building so the uniformed driver, standing guard with a pump shotgun beside Haines' sleek black Chrysler Airflow, didn't see him. As he rode down the elevator, X looked again at the invitation to the ride of a lifetime, the ride to stay alive.

It was signed in the florid hand of Elias Montrose himself. X recognized the signature as genuine; he had spent the previous two days studying Montrose and his dealings in the public and private sectors. He was worth more than Andrew Carnegie and the Rockefeller clan combined, if the intelligence were correct. And in the past three years, he had spent three hundred million dollars on his pet project, the super dirigible Delos.

Closer to a floating hotel than a floating mansion, the three-story gondola could house and feed seventy people including the crew, and stay aloft for weeks at a time before refueling. Since the revelation that The Virus dissipated at high altitudes, Montrose had taken refuge there, floating above it all, and now he was offering asylum to a select few with money and power to barter.

When the elevator doors opened on the lobby, X could hear the sound of rioting close by. As he opened the heavy glass door to step onto the sidewalk, a brick crashed through it, narrowly missing his head, and spraying him with shards of glass.

A screaming man, half his face a raw horror ran at him swinging a long piece of pipe. A step before he got within reach, the blast of a shotgun took the other side of his face from his skull and he fell to the pavement. Archie, thought X, the driver's name is Archie. The uniformed driver ran to X's side and stepped between him and another rioter to club the attacker down with the butt of the shotgun.

"Get in the car, sir," Archie shouted.

X opened the rear door and threw in his bag. He turned in time to see a crazed man with a fire axe running toward Archie from behind as Archie fired a blast that knocked down two more rioters. "Archie, look out!" X drew his revolver and fired into the axe man's chest. The axe clattered to the sidewalk and Archie jumped into the Airflow, and it roared away from the curb, scattering rioters like ninepins. Rocks and bottles clattered off the roof and trunk of the car until it was around the corner and speeding down the next block.

"Are you all right, Mister Haines?"

"Yes, Archie. And you?"

"I'm alive, thanks to you."

"That goes both ways, I think."

"Where are we going, sir?" Archie said as he dodged a burning, over-turned car.

"Across the river, Kensington Airfield."

"Yes, sir." If Archie begrudged or even envied his employer's chance at escape, it showed neither in his voice nor his expression. The chauffeur set his jaw and steered the heavy sedan through the swelling chaos that Manhattan had become.

The streets were alive with swirling masses of people, some running from danger, some running to embrace it. People ran like lunatics cradling pilfered spoil from shattered storefronts. Two men carried a Philco cabinet radio almost as tall as they. Another wild eyed looter shoved a wheeled rack of dresses up the street, bowling over anyone in his path.

A man carrying a box that obscured his vision bounced off the fender of the Chrysler as it sped down the street. He spun two full turns before he fell over his own feet and crashed to the sidewalk. Two screaming men tugged at a case of whiskey until it fell from their grasp and the bottles shattered on the concrete. One of them sat down on the curb and wept. His rival picked up a brick and stoved in the side of his head with it.

Archie slowed to round a corner, and a rioter in a tattered police tunic jumped onto the hood of the car, aiming a revolver through the windshield. "Stop!" he shouted. "Stop in the name of the law!" Archie slammed on the brakes, and the man slid forward, clawing at the hood. Archie rammed his foot on the gas pedal and the man's face disappeared. The car bumped over him like bad pavement, and shot down the street away from the flames and death of the neighborhood.

"I'm not even trying for the tunnels, Mister Haines. At 103rd, there's a double-track railroad trestle. It'll be a rough ride, but this car has enough clearance to make it. We used to drive it hauling bootlegged hooch before Repeal."

"I'll trust your judgment, Archie," said X. "Just get me to Jersey."

Driving through the gap between the trestle's twin sets of tracks was all Archie said it would be. Despite the heavy suspension and oversized tires of the Airflow, every tie they rumbled over jarred X's teeth to the root. If he had rolled down the window, X could have looked down into the dark waters of the Hudson River between the crosshatching of girders, ties, and rails. He prayed that they wouldn't meet an oncoming train.

Across the river, the car lurched over the rails and down a steep embankment into a vacant lot. Archie plowed through the weeds and rubbish to pull out onto a darkened street lined with warehouses. "It's not far now, sir. Looks quiet here." No sooner did the words leave his mouth than a dark bulk rolled from an alleyway between two buildings. It was a stake side truck with a mob of men pushing it across the street as a barricade.

Archie stood on the brake pedal but couldn't avoid slamming into the truck. In seconds, the mob was pounding on the windows of the car with pipes and bricks. The engine was still running, so Archie threw the transmission into reverse. The rear tires spun, shrieking and smoking, but the front fenders had dug into the tires and the best the Airflow could do was drag itself slowly backward like a crippled animal.

One of the mob smashed through the passenger window and tried to climb into the driver's seat. Archie smashed the butt of the shotgun into his forehead and the man lay half-in, half-out of the car, blocking others from entry.

A groan of metal told X that one of the rioters was using a crowbar to pry open one of the back doors. It swung open, and as men swarmed into one door, X rolled out of the other, pistol in one hand and his valise in the other. The shotgun roared one last time, and X heard Archie scream as the mob fell upon him in the close arena of the driver's seat. One of the attackers burst from the rear door, and X shot him before he could say, "There's one of them."

Gasoline. X smelled gasoline. He pulled a handful of matches from his pocket, struck them all on the pavement, and threw them under the Chrysler. The gas tank exploded in a ball of flame, and more than one of the mob staggered away from it afire from head to toe. X ran; the heat at his back and ducked into a darkened alley. Which way to the airfield? How far?

Then he heard it, the drone of motors. Looking up between the buildings, he saw the running lights of a twin-engine plane swooping downward. The field must be close. He set off at a dead run in the direction of the sound and hoped he was not too late.

Four blocks and around a corner, X saw a wooden fence, and beyond it, the lights of a runway. It was Kensington Field. He scrambled over the fence, and ran toward the lights of the closest hangar. As he got closer, he saw the sign over its bay doors: Hunnicutt. A plane sat in front of the hangar, engines running and props idly spinning. He remembered Haines' watch. Seven fifty-five.

He'd made it, but did his disguise still hold after the fighting and running? Two men with Thompson machine guns saw him coming and raised their weapons. "Halt," said the taller of the two. "Identify yourself."

X made a quick decision. While he was still in shadow, he quickly wound his scarf around the lower part of his face. He raised his hands and said, "I am Robert Haines of Consolidated Firearms. I am expected."

"Why didn't you come through the gate?"

"Because my car was waylaid by rioters. My driver was killed. The car burned." X looked over his shoulder. "You can still see the glow from the fire."

He took the last few steps into the light of the hangar. "I am going to reach into my pocket and pull out my invitation from Elias Montrose." X held the envelope at arm's length and the shorter guard lowered his gun and took it from him.

He opened the envelope and read the note inside it. "We'll have to see your face, sir," he said, reaching for the scarf.

X stepped back. "I wouldn't if I were you, son. I've moved past simple plague-sweat. If you touch me, who knows what may happen to you."

The shorter guard stepped back as if he were slapped. X lowered the scarf carefully, keeping most of his face in shadow.

The tall one said, "Are you carrying any weapons, sir?"

"Yes. There is a pistol in each of my coat pockets."

"You'll have to surrender them before you get on the aircraft, sir. Please take them out of your pockets and lay them on the ground."

"Very well." X reached both hands into his pockets.

"One at a time, please. Left hand first."

At that moment shouting came from behind X. Four of the surviving attackers from the warehouse district came running across the field. "There he is," one shouted. "Get him," cried another.

The guards raised their machine guns and with a short burst of fire, dropped all four of the men.

"So you see," X said. He laid his pistols on the tarmac.

"Sorry we doubted you, Mister Haines," said the shorter guard. "You understand the need for security."

"Of course. No offense taken."

"Follow us, please."

In a moment, X was climbing the rollaway ramp into the idling airplane. Outside, the plane looked ordinary. Inside, it resembled nothing so much as the smoking room of a posh men's club. Leather armchairs and a sofa replaced the standard seating. A bar stood at the cockpit end of the cabin, and a closed area aft suggested a private compartment, possibly with a berth and a washroom.

A pretty young woman in a stewardess uniform took his bag and set it inside a cabinet near the cockpit. "If you will have a seat, sir, we'll be taking off in a few minutes. Can I get you anything? A drink perhaps?"

"Yes. A Manhattan, please." Haines' drink of choice. X loosened the scarf and turned his face toward the dark window to study his reflection. He was in luck. The moustache held and the false nose was only slightly askew.

The stewardess returned with his drink. Shall I take your coat, Mister Haines?"

X smiled. "Yes, young lady. He slipped out of his coat and hat and handed them to her. In turn, she handed him his drink. The drink testified to her skill as a bartender. He sipped at it as the plane took off, careful to not dribble a drop and dissolve the spirit gum that held his false chin in place.

X X X

Watching the lights below from the cabin window, X was able to determine that the plane was flying North immediately after takeoff. When he was alone in the cabin for a moment, he carefully twisted the second button of his topcoat clockwise. The button cap was reverse threaded instead of the normal configuration to prevent accidental discovery of the hiding place.

Under the button was a small compass. As they flew over a patch of city lights, X oriented himself and determined that the plane was on a northwest heading. Flying into Canada, he thought. That would be the first leg of a flight to the base Montrose had established on the polar ice cap years before. The rationale for the base was to provide a cleaner environment for research, one with fewer microbes to contaminate experimental cultures, and isolation in case a germ or bacterium escaped the lab. Or a virus, X thought.

The engines droned, and X settled back into the comfortable armchair. He read a magazine from a rack of the latest titles beside his chair, an issue of *Life* with a picture of troops in gas masks guarding a government research center.

An hour into the flight, X closed his eyes and pretended to doze. The pretty young stewardess crept up beside him, and opening his eye a crack, he saw her quickly but carefully search his valise. She would find nothing without the use of a fluoroscope or an X-ray machine because the bag was constructed with more undetectable compartments than he had buttons on his suit.

Satisfied, she closed the bag and tiptoed away to report to her superior. X smiled at her retreating back. He had anticipated that his bag would be searched, and even his person, but he was equipped for almost anything that he might encounter on the Delos, and it would take someone as highly trained as he to find the weapons and devices hidden in the bag.

The plane landed twice to refuel, and each time, as it took off, X noted the heading on his compass. The third landing took place on a field surrounded by a uniform carpet of white. They were in Northern Canada now, and the takeoff heading was due north, as X suspected it would be, leading the flight to the polar ice cap to rendezvous with the zeppelin. Nothing to do now but wait, he thought, and X closed his eyes, this time to really sleep. He would need all his energy, mental and physical, when he boarded the Delos.

X X X

The airplane landed hours later on a bumpy airstrip lit only by lines of flares that defined the runway. Looking out the window, X realized that the strip was solid ice and inwardly congratulated the pilot for his control of the plane.

A vehicle on treads instead of tires was waiting when he disembarked. The driver wore a parka with a furred hood pulled close around his face. X soon learned why. The Arctic cold was punishing on that short ride, and as he wrapped his scarf tightly around his face, X realized that left alone in that dark waste, he could easily die in a half hour or less.

Doors opened, and the crawler drove into a hangar-sized Quonset hut. The temperature difference was dramatic once the doors closed. Inside, a crew was loading crates onto a flatbed truck. Four full-sized fuel trucks waited in a corner of the hut. One other thing he noticed was a pair of men just inside the doors holding Thompson machine guns. Montrose's security was consistent.

The driver shed his parka, and led X to the back of the hut to a makeshift cubicle where a cot, a table, and a chair were waiting. "Please make yourself comfortable, Mister Haines," the driver said. "The Delos will arrive very soon."

X stepped into the room and set down his bag. As he took off his over-coat, the driver closed the door behind him, and X heard the click of a lock. He had no doubt he was being watched through some spyhole in the wall, so he sat in the chair and reached into the inside pocket of his suit. He took out a silver case and selected one of the cigars inside. X lit it and wondered as he puffed at the tobacco, what possessed a man as wealthy as Robert Haines to smoke such cheap, wretched cigars.

By the time X had smoked the cigar to a stub, it was time to leave. The door opened, and another man in a parka and a goggled mask said, "If you'll follow me, please, Mister Haines, and put on your coat and hat. You'll need them." He offered to take X's bag, and X nodded. No need to arouse suspicion.

The weak light of a polar dawn cast the ice cap in shades of blue and grey. X stepped outside the Quonset hut, and was totally unprepared for what greeted him.

He had seen pictures of the Delos before but no photograph could capture the enormity of the super zeppelin he saw moored at the tether. Its great bulk was the size of four football fields, corner to corner, and its gondola looked like a three-story office building, hanging from the great airship's belly. Twelve propellers ringed the gondola, four on each of the long sides, and two at either end.

X's mouth hung open in awe despite himself. The attendant took his arm. "This way, sir." He led X to the bottom of a conveyor with escalator-like treads hauling the crates he'd seen earlier into the ship. The conveyor stopped. "Do you suffer vertigo, Mister Haines?"

"Uh, no," X replied.

"Very good. Then please step onto the conveyor and hold onto the crate in front of you." Haines stepped onto one of the treads and his valise was set on the one behind him. The conveyor resumed with a mild jerk, and carried the agent upward toward the lighted square of the Delos' cargo hatch. The bitter gusts of wind nearly blew X's hat away, but he didn't want to risk letting go of his hand holds to keep it on his head.

At the top of the conveyor, X found himself in a cargo hold not un-like that of a freighter, but one whose entry was in the floor of the hold, not the ceiling. Here too, the armed guards stood by, guns at the ready. Both looked like thugs, as opposed to military personnel. X wondered whether they were really needed, or whether they were for show to make Montrose's guests feel safer.

A man in a grey suit came forward and offered his hand to X. "How do

you do, Mister Haines? I am George Tyrell, Mister Montrose's personal
secretary." Tyrell was one of those short men who tried to make up for his
height with the volume of his voice. "Welcome aboard the Delos. I'll take
you to your quarters. I imagine you're tired after the flight, let alone your
trouble getting out of the city."

X nodded. "Yes, I am tired. Very tired. I could use some rest."

Tyrell smiled, showing a perfectly capped set of teeth. "Right this way,
sir. Oh, and would you put these on, please?" He handed X a pair of white
cotton gloves. "Until your symptoms subside."

Tyrell led him up a spiral staircase to the next level. Crew quarters and
guest cabins lined a long hallway. "Crew compartments are to the inside,
and guest staterooms are to the outside. Most guests prefer windows."

X followed Tyrell past doors with shining gilt numbers like suites in a
hotel. Finally, they arrived at number 17. "Here we are." Tyrell pulled back
his sleeve to reveal an oversized brass key cuffed to his wrist to unlock the
door.

It swung inward to reveal a cozy stateroom not unlike a first-class cabin on an ocean liner. The room was fitted with a swing-down berth, a
writing desk with a gooseneck lamp and a small radio on it. To the left of
the desk was a leather armchair. An open closet and drawers were built
into the wall between the berth and the door to a small washroom. The
floor was carpeted in a rich forest green, matching curtains drawn over a
double window.

"Make yourself comfortable, Mister Haines. If you require anything,
just press the ivory button over the desk to summon an attendant. If you
like, send for me when you're ready, and I'll show you around the ship."

"I'd like to get a message to my office. Is there a way I can do that?"

"Of course. Simply write the message down, give it to Thomas or one
of the other attendants, and we will have the radio room send a telegram
for you."

X nodded, thinking, *and control the flow of information to and from the
ship*. "And when will I meet with Elias Montrose?"

Tyrell smiled again. "This evening at dinner, sir. Mr. Montrose is very
busy at the moment. Ah, here is your bag." A tall man in the white waist-
length jacket of a bellhop or waiter stood at the door with the Gladstone
bag in his hand. "Set it over there, please, Thomas."

"I'm very glad you are here, Mister Haines," Tyrell said. "And Mister
Montrose is pleased as well. Have a good rest." Tyrell closed the door, leaving X alone. He waited for the click of the lock and heard none. He could

"I'm very happy you are here, Mr. Haines."

move around the airship with relative freedom. A brass key like the one Tyrell used hung by the door. It was stamped with the number 17. Tyrell's key is likely a master key, X thought. That could come in handy later.

He heard a muffled clank and felt rather than heard the throb of heavy motors. X drew open the curtains and saw the ground below slip away as the giant dirigible rose from its tether. The higher the ship rose, the further the expanse of ice and snow unfolded before X's eyes. He could see snow squalls a hundred miles away, and banks of clouds like mountain ranges spreading into the distance. Above it all, Delos floated like one of those clouds, smooth, fluid, peaceful. Whatever else Elias Montrose may have done, X thought, no one could disparage the achievement the Delos represented.

X secured the cabin door with an inside deadbolt and opened the berth. It was just shy of a double bed and could probably sleep two people comfortably. Questions raced through his mind, and he felt the humming tension of the tightrope he was walking, but without sleep, he would be good to no one. He stretched out on the bed, face up so as to not disturb his disguise, and fell quickly to sleep.

X X X

Four hours later, X rang for service and Thomas answered the call. X noticed that his head and shoulders barely cleared the door frame of the cabin. He also noticed the bulge of a holster under Thomas's jacket. Whatever Montrose was up to, he was prepared for trouble.

"If Mister Tyrell isn't too busy at the moment, I'd like to take him up on his offer of seeing the ship."

"Very good, sir." He looked past X to the rumpled suit hanging on the rack beside the washroom. "Shall I have your suit pressed?"

"Yes, I'd like that. I want to look my best to meet Mister Montrose."

Thomas folded the suit over his arm. "I'll notify Mister Tyrell, and he should be here shortly."

X was wearing a pair of wool trousers, a navy blue turtleneck sweater, and a pair of black steel-toed shoes. The outfit was copied from a photo of Robert Haines taken on the floor of the Consolidated Arms factory. He opened one of the drawers. In it was the suit jacket he had worn on the flight. The coat Thomas had taken was identical except for the hidden weapons. Once it was returned, he could wear the original without suspicion.

X checked the cigars in his case. Two held small explosive charges, a third, a small tear gas cartridge. He turned these so the gold bands were label down. As he slipped the case into his shirt pocket, a knock came at the door. It was Tyrell.

As they left the stateroom, X noticed a deadbolt on the outside of the door identical to that on the inside. He could lock others out, but they also could lock him in. The secretary led X to the end of the corridor where it made a left turn, and took them to another spiral staircase. He noticed a second hallway, parallel to his own. "More staterooms?"

"Yes, another set identical to your corridor." Tyrell climbed the stair and X followed him to Deck 3. The stairs opened into a spacious, well-lit area with a bar and tables laid out like a restaurant. The outside wall was more glass than not, and afforded a spectacular panorama of sky and clouds. ""We call this the Sky Room. It's our dining area and general gathering place." At one table, four men sat playing poker, mounds of chips in front of them. At another, a man X recognized as the controlling stockholder of the National Agriculture Corporation was engaged in a game of backgammon with the Owner of Municipal Tool and Die. Three other men sat engaged in an earnest discussion over drinks.

A quick glance told X that the bar was well-stocked. "The kitchen is behind that wall," Tyrell said. I think you will find the cuisine quite good."

Beyond the Sky Room, to the left lay a smoking room appointed with every comfort, and a well-stocked library. A billiard table sat in one corner. Noticing his attention, Tyrell said, "It's on very responsive gimbals and remains level even in low grade turbulence. Mister Montrose designed it himself." The floor also offered a small gymnasium equipped with a rowing machine and pulley weights. "We don't have anything loose to roll around and crash through the walls," Tyrell said with a laugh, "but our guests seem to find the equipment adequate. Shower stalls are through that door."

They returned to the Sky Room and X asked, "What's past the other end of this room?"

Tyrell pointed to a door beside the staircase. "Through that door is Mister Montrose's private suite, his living quarters and the office where he conducts business."

"What's through there?" X pointed through the kitchen doorway to a door that had a heavier than usual lock.

"That leads upstairs to the hull of the ship, the 'bag-room' as Mister Montrose calls it. He said that he'd like to show you the 'nuts and bolts' of the ship personally, both of you being designers and engineers."

"I'll look forward to it," X said.

"Dinner is at eight o'clock. I'll leave you to look around. Make your-self at home, Mister Haines." Tyrell gave X his perfect smile, unlocked Montrose's private door with his master key, and slipped through it like a shadow.

X stepped to the bar, and the bartender stepped over. "Good afternoon, Mister Haines. Welcome to Delos. Shall I fix you a Manhattan?" X was not surprised that the bartender knew his pretended name and favorite drink. What he found curious was that he recognized the dark-haired bartender by his long nose and deep set eyes. He was Charles "Charlie the Chopper" Bardini, a hit man for the Mob with a reputed fourteen kills in his career. His nickname came from his habit of cutting the trigger fingers from his victims.

"Yes," X said, hiding his surprise. "I'd like a Manhattan–uh, what's your name young man?"

"Charles," Bardini said with a lopsided grin. "Most people just call me Charlie."

"Charlie it is."

X took his drink to a table by the window wall and looked beyond a bed of clouds at the bluest sky he'd ever seen. In the distance, the sun glinted off the silver fuselage of an airplane flying the other direction.

"Hello, Bob, I wondered when you'd show up." A large man with a bald head and rimless glasses that magnified his green eyes almost comically sat beside him.

"Hello, Ernie." X recognized Ernie Watson, the owner and president of Midwest Petroleum.

"You're the last."

"Last?"

"Last of the Wall Street Thirty to arrive. I guess you just got here," he said, pointing his chin toward X's gloves. "The others have arrived over the past week."

"Is it true that the altitude destroys The Virus?"

Ernie dragged his palm across the white linen table cloth, leaving no mark. "Clean as a whistle; Don't need the gloves anymore, and I've only been here three days. Can't complain about the accommodations, either."

"No, the service seems first-rate."

Ernie swirled the ice in his highball. "I don't see any of Montrose's competitors here. I guess it would suit him just fine if they all died of The

Virus." He leaned in close. "And I wonder why Montrose is being so generous with all of us. He doesn't give anything away."

"I guess we'll find out before too long."

Watson got up to get another highball, and X took the opportunity to
leave the Sky Room with a wave and a "see you later" to Watson. The less
detailed his conversations with people who knew Haines, the better.

Returning to his stateroom, X gave the pretense of casual curiosity as
he strolled around the upper level of the Delos. On the side opposite the
Sky Room he found an open balcony complete with deck chairs on the
other side of a window wall. When he tried the door handle, X found it
was locked.

"I'm sorry, sir. When we're flying in the upper altitudes, especially in
this region, the temperatures are far too cold for anyone to go into the
open air."

X turned to see another attendant dressed like Thomas behind him. If
the fellow was tailing him, he was pretty good. "Oh, right. I didn't even
think about that."

"The balcony will be available in a day or two when we're over warmer
territory, sir." The attendant walked past X and disappeared down the corridor.

When he returned to the second floor, X tried the handle of the door
that led to the staircase and into the lower section of the gondola. It too
was locked, as were most of the doors on the ship. Back in his cabin, he sat
at the desk and took a close look at the radio.

He turned it on and dialed around the bands, finding mostly static.
He finally found a station playing big band music. The announcer spoke
French, so X figured it was broadcasting from Quebec. He gently removed
the screws from the back of the radio and held it to the light of the desk
lamp. Inside was a soldered connection to a tiny microphone. The radio
was a surveillance device.

X smiled. He could disable the microphone, but that would alert the
guards that he knew about it. The radio was a two-edged sword. He could
not use own his own short wave transmitter without being overheard, unless he masked the sound with music from the desktop unit; maybe in the
washroom. If the guards relied on the hidden microphone to know when
he was in the room, that meant they weren't doing constant eyes-on surveillance, something he could use to his advantage.

He turned the volume of the music a little higher and opened his bag.
He took out his makeup kit and went into the washroom, closing the door

behind him. Plague-sweat made it necessary to be more watchful than usual with his disguise, but if what Watson said was accurate, it would soon cease to be a problem. Satisfied, X replaced the kit and lay on the berth face up. Better to sleep now for the night ahead, but he never got the chance. Someone knocked at the door of his cabin. "Mister Haines?" X recognized the voice as Tyrell. "Mister Montrose would like to see you if it's convenient."

X opened the door and stepped into the corridor. He paused. "Should I lock the door?"

Tyrell smiled. "Whatever you prefer."

"Oh, what the hell, there's nothing much in there anyway. And if someone stole something on this ship, where would he take it?"

Tyrell laughed. "Quite right. This way, Mister Haines."

As he followed Tyrell, X studied the man carefully. He seemed to be one of the few of Montrose's men who wasn't carrying a gun. Tyrell led him to the third floor and the Sky Room, where the window wall opened onto a spectacular Polar sunset. "Through here, sir." Tyrell opened the door to Montrose's quarters, and gestured for X to follow.

X found himself in another hallway and at its end, a door covered in red leather. It swung open, and X stepped into a half-circle room at the very front of the gondola. Floor to ceiling windows gave the illusion that he was floating in the sky. The room was a conservatory, filled with green plants of every description, tastefully arranged so as to not block the remarkable view.

"Magnificent, isn't it?"

X turned to see a man he recognized as Elias Montrose sitting in an armchair at perfect ease, legs crossed, ankle over knee, a snifter of brandy in one hand and a cigar in the other. A thick shock of white hair cascaded over his boulder of a forehead and a pair of deep set slate-colored eyes. Lines around his eyes and framing his mouth testified to his age, but the presence and power the man radiated as he rose from the chair were that of a man in his prime. He was wearing canvas dungarees and a Pendleton wool shirt as if he were in a hunting lodge rather than an elegant salon.

"The view, I mean, not the ship." He set down his brandy and cigar and stepped forward offering his hand. "I'm happy to meet you in person, Mister Haines. Elias Montrose."

"Yes, the view is spectacular," X said looking once again at the blood red snowscape. He shook hands with Montrose, whose grip equaled his own. "Please, call me Bob."

"In time." Montrose cast a gaze through the glass at the dying sun. "Do you know the work of Frank Lloyd Wright?"

"The architect? Yes, I've seen pictures of his buildings."

"Buildings?" Montrose scoffed. "They're masterpieces, works of art." He crossed the room and pulled an oversized book from a shelf near the door. "Have you seen Fallingwater?"

"The house cantilevered over a waterfall? As I said, I've seen pictures."

"Do you know that he designed Fallingwater specifically so that the waterfall couldn't be seen from inside the house?" He opened the book to a marked page and turned it toward X. It showed Fallingwater from below, including the rocky cascade that poured from beneath the house. "He didn't want the sight of the waterfall to become so commonplace that the owners lost appreciation for it. That's why I usually keep the curtains closed. Then every time I come in here and open them, it's like unwrapping a gift."

The men stood silent for a full minute, gazing at the scene thousands of feet below. Then Montrose stepped to the wall and pressed a control button. The drapes glided silently over the glass, and the sunset was gone. "So, Mister Haines, what do you think of the Delos so far?" The steely grey eyes bored into X's, taking his measure.

X smiled. "From what I've seen, it's almost as spectacular as that sunset. Of course, I haven't seen the whole ship yet."

Montrose chuckled without smiling. "A good diplomatic answer, and one with motive, fishing for the invitation. And see the rest you shall." He led X back into the corridor where Tyrell waited like a faithful dog. He handed Montrose two sheets of paper. Montrose read the first and gave it back to Tyrell with a shake of his head. He read the second and drew a gold fountain pen from the pocket of his Pendleton and scrawled a few lines on the bottom of the page. He handed the second sheet to Tyrell, who nodded and hurried off to do his master's bidding.

"What you have seen so far," Montrose said, "is what all of my guests have seen, the luxury liner amenities, the trappings of comfort. What I am about to show you, Mister Haines, are the hidden gears and shafts and cams that make the merry-go-round whirl. As an engineer and designer, you are uniquely suited to appreciate what I have accomplished here."

Montrose led X to a door that opened onto another spiral staircase. "Do you know why I named the ship Delos?"

"After the fabled floating island?"

Montrose nodded. "Very good. You know your Classical mythology, Mister Haines."

"All part of a well-rounded Duquesne education."

"You'd be surprised how few people recognize the allusion."

The stair descended past the second deck and directly into the bridge of the ship. Five uniformed men sat at various control panels monitoring instruments, scribbling calculations, and operating controls. "This is the command center where all systems are monitored and operated.

"Captain Willet," Montrose said, and a tall lean man with gold bars on his epaulets rose from one of the panels of dials and gauges. "This is Mister Robert Haines. Could you please give him a brief overview of the bridge and its operation. He's an engineer; feel free to speak technically."

"Yes sir." He turned to another officer. "Compton, take the helm." The Captain spoke with an upper-crust British accent, and his military bearing gave X the impression that he was ex-RAF. Willet swept his arm in an encompassing gesture. "Twin diesel engines, two thousand horsepower each, are the heart of the Delos, this room is her brain. The instrument consoles monitor every mechanical and electrical function, as well as atmospheric conditions outside the ship." he pointed to a device like a stock ticker in a corner of the bridge. "That gives regular weather reports from a hundred mile radius of the ship's position."

"So you can avoid storms?"

"Yes, and simply float in pleasant conditions to conserve fuel without being turned about by the wind." Willet stepped to the helm, which consisted of an oversized joystick projecting from the floor. "This is the master control to steer the Delos. You noticed that the gondola is ringed with propellers?"

X nodded. "Twelve, correct?"

"Yes. Four on each side, two fore and two aft. How familiar are you with physics, Mister Haines?"

"I'm conversant with its principles."

"Then you understand the concept of vectors; directed force will push an object in one direction." He pushed his left hand forward. "Multiple directed forces applied simultaneously will determine the direction of the object's movement based on force." He pushed his left hand forward again, but this time, he pressed it from the side with his right, veering it from its path. "By accelerating specific propellers and slowing or even reversing others like oars in a rowboat, we are able to maneuver the ship much more efficiently than by any rudder."

"And the joystick?"

"It coordinates the propeller operation to give the right mix of fast and slow, forward and reverse."

"But the ship does have a rudder as well?"

"Two in fact," said Willet, "to assist stabilization in high winds."

"The whole operation is impressive," said X. "How many people are required to man the bridge?"

"Five in full flight," Montrose answered, "and when we're just drifting, three. Plus the sentries, of course."

"Ever worry about collision with an airplane?"

Montrose laughed. "I don't find that very likely. There's not much traffic at this altitude. As big as the Delos is, I don't think anyone could help but see her, even at night with the running lights on. As for an intentional collision, it would be a suicide mission."

"I see what you mean."

"Would you like to try the helm, sir?" Willet offered.

"Who wouldn't?"

"Just take the stick. I recommend both hands for steadiness."

X took the stick and felt the vibration of motors and mechanisms pulsing through it into his palms.

"Now, use the rotating compass mounted in front of you as a guide. We need to adjust our heading fifteen degrees to the southwest. Simply push the stick and watch the needle."

X pushed the stick to his left and felt the vibration change. He found that steering the Delos was like steering an ocean liner, but much easier. He intentionally overshot the mark then corrected it to get the feel of the control.

"Very good, sir. I'll take it from here."

"Come, Mister Haines," said Montrose. "Now that you've seen the brain of the ship, let me show you its heart." X followed him past the open door of the radio room down a narrow corridor. Montrose used his master key to open a heavy door, and as soon as he did, the thrum of engines poured through the doorway.

"Twin diesels at 2,000 horsepower plus," Montrose said, raising his voice to be heard. "And at the rear of the gondola, an auxiliary engine for emergency power."

"That's little more than the Hindenberg had."

"And all that we need given the economical mechanics of the Delos' construction and propulsion system."

Unlike engine rooms X had seen on ships, crusted with grease and stained with oil, the engines of the Delos were gleaming and spotlessly clean. "Magnetos driven by the engines generate enough current to light a small town. And beyond the engines, you see the gyroscopes made to my specifications by the Sperry Corporation." Montrose pointed to a pair of huge wheels rotating on vertical axles. "Are you familiar with the principle?"

X feigned ignorance. "I've heard the word, but I don't really know how they work."

"The gyros' rotation stabilizes the ship, holds it level. Otherwise, suffice to say that in heavy turbulence we might tilt back and forth like a porch swing."

At the door beyond the gyroscopes, X saw another armed guard. "I've noticed that you have armed men in several key locations, everywhere except the passenger quarters and the Sky Room. Are they really necessary? I would think that no one could cause a row up here. It's a long way down."

Montrose smiled. "Humans are unpredictable, and we're all dealing with the survival of ourselves and the race. This ship is a means to preserve the intellectual and financial seed grain of the future. It is for that reason, worth protecting."

"Some of the guards look pretty rough, almost like thugs."

"Most of them are, Mister Haines. Our government needs all the soldiers and policemen they have to maintain order. I had to settle for what professionals I could find, mercenaries, soldiers of fortune, and in a few cases, people of less savory origins. They are perfectly devoted to me; no better inspiration for loyalty than the chance to live while so many others are dying."

"I get your point. I haven't seen any women on board."

"You'll see them later. If you want one, I'll have Tyrell bring her to you."

X let that offer go by without an answer. They passed a steel cabinet marked PARACHUTES. "I've seen those at different locations. Do you have them all over the ship?"

Montrose nodded. "You are very observant, Mister Haines. Yes, in the event of an emergency, I felt it was better to have parachutes in locations where everyone, passengers and crew could reach them quickly rather than having a mob scene in a central location."

"So instead of lifeboat drills—"

"We have parachute drills. You'll experience one tomorrow."

"Wouldn't I find thin air and freezing cold at this altitude?"

"If we need to abandon the Delos, it will be at a much lower altitude than we normally fly."

They had reached the end of the lowest level, and through a line of windows, X saw a winged shape mounted just beyond the glass. "It's an airplane."

"No, it's a glider. It will carry me and one other person."

"No 'Captain going down with the ship,' eh?"

"That is a foolish notion at best."

Montrose led X up a series of stairs beyond the upper level of the gondola. He paused at the top before unlocking the door and turning the wheel that secured it. "You mentioned the Hindenberg. Didn't that tragedy give you pause before coming on board the Delos?"

"I admit I had mixed feelings, but I assumed that you were no fool and wouldn't put yourself at undue risk."

Montrose laughed again. "Clever answers. I like you more all the time, Mister Haines. Follow me." He opened the door and X found himself standing on a narrow catwalk that stretched the two hundred yards of the upper frame. On either side and overhead hundreds of gas bags bulged like enormous tawny breasts.

Montrose opened his cigarette case and took out a Turkish Oval. "Cigarette, Mister Haines?"

"Isn't that a little dangerous up here?"

"Not at all." Montrose lit his cigarette with a flick of a gold plated Zippo lighter. The bags are filled with an inert gas, helium, not inflammable hydrogen."

"Isn't helium very rare?"

"It is, relative to other gases, but when money is no object. . . ." His voice trailed off.

"Why so many gas bags?"

"Ah, you noticed one of the most important features of the design." He swept his arm in a broad gesture. "The outer skin of the Delos is rubberized canvas stretched over an extruded aluminum frame. Inside that skin, two hundred thirty expandable balloons filled with helium. Each has its own compression cylinder of gas. Compressed, helium is dense and heavy. Let out of the cylinders into the bags, it expands and buoys the ship. Pump the helium back into the storage cylinders, and it compresses once again, forcing the ship to a lower altitude."

"Remarkable." And X was sincere in his compliment. He turned and saw Tyrell leaning on the railing at the end of the catwalk.

"Tyrell will show you back to your quarters, Mister Haines. I hope you have enjoyed the tour."

"Very much."

"I'll see you this evening at dinner." Montrose turned away and strolled down the catwalk as casually as he might on a pathway through Central Park.

Tyrell was at X's elbow, smiling . "This way, Mister Haines."

Back in his stateroom, X played the table radio to cover the sound of his actions. Under the false bottom of his valise, he found the tiny short wave transmitter. He chose a frequency far above routine radio bands and quickly tapped out a coded message with the red button built into the side of the unit. X didn't wait for acknowledgment, realizing what a risk he was taking. The message was simple: *on board accepted.*

He immediately replaced the transmitter and stretched out on the cot, waiting. No footsteps, no knock at the door, no men with guns bursting into the stateroom. His transmission either went unnoticed, or it was over too quickly for the radio room to get a fix on its source. So far so good.

Whatever Montrose is up to, he hasn't shown his cards yet, X thought. I'll find out more at dinner tonight. In the meantime, I may as well enjoy the comfort.

X X X

Seven o'clock came quickly, and X found he was hungrier than he would have expected. Must be the altitude, he thought. A quick check of his disguise, and X sat in the armchair with a magazine until a knock came at the stateroom door. Through the panel, Thomas said, "It is time for dinner, Mister Haines. Please come to the Sky Room," and moved on to the next door.

X stepped into the corridor and saw men leaving their compartments. Some wore suits and ties, but most were in casual cold weather gear, pullover sweaters and wool shirts. He followed the crowd up the spiral stairs to the upper deck and found that the Sky Room's tables had been reconfigured from a night club setup to something approximating a banquet arrangement.

Eddie waved him over to an empty chair, but X ignored him and sat with a group of men he recognized as bankers and financiers, people less likely to know Robert Haines as well as the industrialists. The table cloths were linen, and the silver and crystal were top shelf. Montrose spared no expense outfitting his flying retreat.

"Would you like chicken or fish, sir?" X recognized the white-jacketed waiter as one of the gun-guards from the ship's hold.

He followed the crowd up the spiral stairs...

"Fish, please."

"Something from the bar for you?"

"Not right now, thank you," X said. As the waiter left the table, X saw the bulge of a holster under his arm.

There was no head table in the Sky Room. Montrose entered as dinner was about to be served and sat at a seemingly random empty chair. He had traded his Pendleton for a navy blue blazer over a green silk shirt—no necktie. The appearance was egalitarian. Montrose is passing himself off as "just one of the guys," X thought, but he's the only one with a squad of gunmen to back his play.

Talk at X's table centered around the latest news of the plague and its effects, panic and riots. "What I want to know is what the damned government is doing about it. They can send all the troops and cops they want to stop rioting and looting, but what good will that do if everyone dies from The Virus? We kept it out of the U.S. for a long time, but now it's here."

"It's not the government that's going to find a cure, it's the private sector," said another.

"Montrose's people are supposed to be working around the clock," a third chimed in. "So are the other pharmaceutical companies and research labs. Everything is being done that can be."

"Well, you know what I think?" the first speaker said. "I think the government's taking advantage of this crisis to put John Q. Public even more under its thumb than it is already. A cure might be found, but who's going to hand it out? The government. And who gets it first? Congress and the Cabinet. And then there'll be so much squabbling over whose district gets it next that most average people will die waiting for decisions to be made."

"That's a really dark vision, Clemmons," said one of the others. "How did you ever become so cynical?"

"Why are we even talking like this?" said a man with a pink face over a red paisley bow tie, a man X recognized as David Kroener, the Chairman of the Board of Universal Aluminum. "We're over the altitude and except for Haines here," he nodded toward X, "who's still wearing gloves, all of us are well on the mend. Let's see a little bit of optimism."

"I'll reserve judgment, Kroener," Clemmons grumbled.

"Well, what do you think is going to happen? That Elias—" he looked over to the table where Montrose sat regaling the five men with him—"is going to walk among us dressed like the Red Death and strike us all down? He's brought us all here to keep us safe until this whole thing blows over and we can go back to making money again."

Clemmons harrumphed and rattled the ice in his drink.

"Here comes dinner."

The food was excellent, from the Caesar salad to the charlotte russe. As everyone was enjoying after dinner drinks and coffee, Montrose stood at his table. "Gentlemen, I trust you've enjoyed your meal. I expect that most of you are keeping up with current events as best you can with the radio, but the press never tells the whole story. This afternoon, I received a report from the head of Montrose Research concerning the ongoing quest to find a cure for The Virus." All chatter in the room ceased.

"I will spare you the pages and pages of statistical data and cut to, as so many of you like to call it, the bottom line. Montrose Laboratories has developed a series of test vaccines that may prevent persons who are not yet infected with The Virus from contracting it. Trials have begun but the vaccines cannot be pronounced effective until we can determine their long-term results. As all of you know, that will take time. Granted, this is not a cure, but it could slow, or even stop the spread of The Virus in America. We are hopeful that this breakthrough will lead to a permanent cure, unlike the altitude.

"In the interim, I suggest that you sit back, relax, light up a Camel," this got chuckles from the group, "or whatever else you smoke, and enjoy the hospitality of the Delos. I am in no rush to rid myself of any of you, but I'm sure we all agree, the sooner we can return to the ground, the better for us all."

The speech got applause from some of the guests, and hard stares from others. Tyrell appeared behind Montrose and spoke in his ear. Montrose excused himself to his table mates and followed Tyrell through the door into his private quarters.

"Well that was informative," said Clemmons with a bitter tinge of sarcasm to his voice.

X glanced at the clock on the wall near the door. He pulled out Haines' pocket watch and was setting it when Kroener said. "What a remarkable fob," as he pointed to the double eagle at the end of the watch chain.

X looked up and smiled. "That's my good luck piece."

"I'm sure there's a story behind it," Kroener said.

"It happened so long ago, that I'm surprised you've never heard it," X said, holding up the pierced gold piece. "How about the rest of you?" Two nodded and the rest shook their heads.

X had read three versions of the story in his research of Robert Haines' past and chose the simplest one to recount. "Eight years ago, my design team had developed a special weapon, an easily concealed, palm-sized pistol with a rotating firing pin that would shoot four .45 caliber shells in quick succession. A prototype was built, and a bench test was arranged. Naturally, I wanted to see the weapon for myself, so I went to the factory for the test firing.

"The technician was fitting the pistol into the test frame when it slipped from his hands and landed on the concrete floor. It discharged and the shot hit me in the leg. I might have lost that leg, or even died, but the bullet struck that double eagle in my pocket." X tapped the coin with a finger. The slug went partway through it, far enough to give me an ugly bruise on my thigh as big as my open hand." X spread his fingers to illustrate.

"My God," said one of the men. "I suppose the coin was good luck at that."

"Indeed," said X, "and I've carried it with me ever since."

"And what about the pistol?"

"We discontinued work on it after that incident. The prototype today hangs in a shadow box in my office at Consolidated as a reminder of how tenuous life can be and how much can depend on the smallest detail any given day."

"Hell of a story."

"And every word of it's true." X handed the watch and chain to Kroener, who looked it over wonderingly and handed to the man next to him. The men passed it around the table and as the last handed it back to X, he said, "Do you still think it's lucky?"

X said, "I'm up here and not down there. Sure, I do."

As the staff cleared the tables in the Sky Room, several of the men went into the smoking room while others went to their cabins. X sat in one of the armchairs with a cigar and leafed through a magazine, listening to bits and snatches of the conversation around him, and filing it all away to process later. In the corner, several men kibitzed while two others played billiards.

"So what do you think, Bob?" It was Ernie Watson. He was on what had to be his third or fourth highball and was more than a little drunk.

"I don't know enough to think anything except that after what I went through last night, I'm glad to be here in one piece." He recounted the riot, the harrowing trip across the railroad bridge, and the attack on the car that killed Archie. "How about you, Ernie?"

"I just drove to the airport and got on the plane." Watson shook his head and walked away to get another drink.

"I hear you got a personal tour of the blimp from Montrose himself." A man sank into the chair beside X. "Ellis Willamette," he said, tipping his glass toward X in salute.

"Houston Diesel," X said. "I believe I've met you once before. A group photo swam into X's memory, Willamette beside him with others and the Secretary of Commerce on the steps of the White House. "It was that event in—D.C. was it?"

"You have a good memory, Haines. It was that National Recovery Administration conference when we were all called in to rah-rah for Roosevelt and his big plans to pull us out of the Depression. A dyed in the wool Republican like me was about as welcome as a rattlesnake to F.D.R., but they needed the appearance of bipartisan support to sell the plan."

"I guess it worked, if only halfway."

"The only thing's going to put the economy back on the rails is another war. In the meantime, we'll just flounder."

"If the plague runs on much longer, will it really matter?"

"No," Willamette said, taking a sip of his bourbon. "Probably not. The only comfort I have is that the other countries got a head start with it. When The Virus is finally under control, and I have every faith that it will be, everybody else will be so far behind they'll be buying from us for decades. Did Montrose tell you that my company built the engines for the Delos?"

X shook his head. "No, he didn't."

"That's because the bastard had them built in Germany. Nice talking to you, Haines." Willamette tipped forward from the overstuffed chair and ambled away.

X stubbed out his cigar and rose from his chair. He decided to go back to his cabin before one of the Wall Street Thirty started a conversation about something he knew nothing about.

He was halfway across the Sky Room when Tyrell came from the kitchen area with a white-jacket rolling a cart with a projector and octagonal canisters of film. Tyrell clapped his hands for attention. "Grab a seat, everyone."

"What's going on?" X said.

"They show movies every night, all the latest."

"What's showing tonight?" one of the guests asked.

"*Too Hot to Handle*, sir," the waiter said. "Clark Gable, Myrna Loy, and Walter Pigeon."

Ernie tugged at X's sleeve. "Aren't you staying for the movie, Bob?"

"Seen it," he said, and headed for the spiral staircase.

Back in the stateroom, X carefully removed his prosthetic chin and peeled away his false moustache. He retrieved the Dopp kit from his valise and brushed up a mug full of lather. He had to shave at least twice a day to prevent stubble from forming under the false chin and loosening it. He crossed his fingers that the altitude cure for The Virus would prevent plague-sweat from accomplishing the same thing.

He had to stay in character twenty-four hours a day because he never knew when an opportunity or an imposition would take him out of his cabin and put him among people who knew Robert Haines at least by sight. So far, he'd gotten away with it, but one slip could be his and the mission's undoing, and depending on what Montrose was up to, there was no telling what he might do with an impostor. He could return him to the Arctic base to find his own way home, or just throw him off the balcony with a parachute—or without one.

After he finished shaving, X replaced the cleft chin and the moustache. Its drooping ends hid the nearly imperceptible edges of the false chin on either side of his mouth, but the bottom edge under the chin always needed careful application. He studied his disguise in the mirror and decided that it was perfect. It seemed almost silly to disguise himself then go to bed, but X had learned through years of hard experience that although he slept, the mission never did.

X X X

What woke X just after dawn was not the sound of the engines, but its absence. He opened the curtains over his berth and in the pale glow of dawn, he saw ice and snow, but he also saw trees and rocks. Tundra; they had moved south overnight. He could see that the ship was not moving faster now than two knots. It was drifting, conserving fuel.

He dressed and climbed the stairs to the Sky Room where breakfast was being served. He saw more or less the same knots of people at the same tables as he had the day before. It hadn't taken long for Montrose's guests to separate into cliques.

A chef, complete with a *toque blanche*, was making omelets to order at a small table near the kitchen door. Bowls of fresh fruit sat at every table, and strong, rich coffee was poured by the waiters from silver carafes.

X stood at the glass wall staring at the wilderness below. He thought, if this is all theater, how long does Montrose intend to continue the performance? How long can this artificial life style be sustained? As one of the guests said earlier, Montrose never gave anything away, and X wondered how soon the "free lunch" would end.

"This flying party boat must cost fifty grand a day," said Willamette, standing beside X and looking through the glass.

"A modern version of Cleopatra's barge," X said.

"You mean Cleopatra as in Marc Antony?"

"She had a barge too, and I'm sure it was a beauty, but I was referring to the pleasure ship built in 1816 by Crowninshield shipbuilders of Massachusetts. I suppose after every war people celebrate with indulgence. It cost a hundred thousand dollars to build and fit, and in today's money, it would have cost millions. It had mahogany paneling, velvet furniture, fine silver and china, and even indoor plumbing. It was the first pure pleasure craft ever to sail across the Atlantic."

"I never figured you to be a history buff, Haines."

X shrugged. "A pastime. I travel so much, or at least I did, that I had plenty of time to read things that interested me."

"Where do you suppose we are now?" Willamette said, changing the subject.

"Based on the landscape, I'd say northern Canada, but which province, I couldn't guess."

"Try the western omelet," Willamette said. "It's pretty good." He turned away and headed for the smoking room. Willamette was right. X's western omelet was done to perfection.

After breakfast, X took a casual stroll around the decks of the Delos, orienting himself and forming a map of the ship's corridors and passageways in his head. The sketchy blueprints published with magazine features about the dirigible barely scratched the surface of its complex layout.

He walked unchallenged through the corridors for at least an hour, but when he strolled in the direction of the bridge on Deck 1, a voice called from behind him, "Excuse me, sir."

X turned to see one of the crewmen, clad in dark shirt and trousers, and a white peaked cap with a black bill. "Yes?"

"I'm afraid that area is off-limits for passengers." His manner was almost apologetic, but X could see in his eyes the cold calculation of a man weighing a potential threat.

"Oh, I'm sorry. I was down here yesterday and thought it was all right to walk around."

"Yes, sir, and if you are accompanied by Mister Montrose or Mister

Tyrell, I am sure you will be welcome on the bridge another time."

"Of course." X nodded and stepped past the crewman. He continued down the corridor for thirty yards and when he turned to look back, the uniformed man still stood in the passageway watching him.

X spent the rest of the morning in the gymnasium, one of the few common rooms where he found privacy. It seemed that most of the businessmen kept exercise at the bottom of their respective agendas. To X, it was a matter of common sense and survival to keep himself in top shape. An added benefit was the relief from tension that hard exercise provided. In an hour, he was sweating profusely, and his muscles ached. A careful shower, and X returned to stateroom 17 to change his clothes for lunch.

He opened the stateroom door and found Thomas standing outside it, his fist poised to knock. "Lunch is being served now, sir."

"Thank you, Thomas." X climbed the stairs to Deck 3 and found the tables in the Sky Room nearly full. Like passengers on an ocean liner, Montrose's guests fell into the meal schedule, eagerly anticipating the next culinary delight. Recreational eating, thought X. What will they do when the beef bourguignon becomes hamburger as supplies get scarce? Or will this adventure last that long? And how long will it take for the novelty of the Delos to wear off and tedium to set in, and with it, irritation and discord? Even staying alive could lose its luster if one is locked in a box too long.

X X X

That evening, X followed the crowd to Deck 3 and the Sky Room for supper. Like lunch, the tables were filled, all but one. A table was set with a single place near the door to Montrose's quarters. It stood empty for the entire meal and X's tablemates speculated about what that meant.

"Do think he's ill?"

"Maybe his company made some breakthrough and he's busy with it."

"That wouldn't explain why he has his own table."

"If it is set for him."

"Who else?

It was not until the after dinner drinks that Montrose finally appeared, dressed in the same clothes that he'd worn the evening before. The smiling Tyrell followed close behind him with a briefcase under one arm.

"Good evening, gentlemen." Montrose strode to the table and stood at his place. "I trust you've enjoyed dinner. As Lewis Caroll put it: "The time has come," the Walrus said, "to talk of many things." But first, allow me to set the scene." He nodded to Tyrell who disappeared through a doorway for a moment and returned with a waiter pushing the projector cart. A screen unrolled from the ceiling at the far end of the room.

The lights in the Sky Room dimmed. In a moment, the projector came to life, reels turning and mechanism ratcheting. A brash fanfare accompanied the familiar Eyes of the World title, the Paramount Studios logo and the clockwise sweep that wiped away one image and replaced it with another on the four corners of the screen, symbolizing the four corners of the Earth..

The newsreel showed mounds of the dead piled in the streets of Asian and African villages, and scenes of rioting in one European city after another, calling The Virus a "medical apocalypse." The film cut to the President from the emergency White House on Mount McKinley. "There is no question," he said, looking into the camera, "that we are facing a grave situation here and abroad, but rest assured that all resources of the public and private sectors are being brought to bear to find a cure for The Virus. In the meantime, I urge all citizens to exercise good judgment and remain calm as we work to resolve this crisis." The film then cut to scenes of rioting and looting in Boston, Los Angeles, and other major cities as, in the words of the newsreel narrator Gregory Abbott, "America descends into chaos."

There was silence for a full minute as Montrose let the impact of the film sink in. "That, gentlemen, is what you have left behind you. Disorder, chaos, and of course, the effects of The Virus. I have offered you sanctuary in an effort to preserve a foundation to restore economy and industry once this crisis has passed."

"You mean 'if the crisis passes,' don't you?" a voice said from a table behind X. "'When' seems to be awfully wishful thinking."

"Mister Travis," Montrose said. "My company and others, as well as the best minds of every university and research facility are working night and day to discover a means to curb and ultimately eradicate The Virus. I have every faith that they will succeed."

Travis rose from his seat. He was a tall man with long arms and hands like baseball gloves. "I accepted your offer of safety, Elias, but I know you too well. You never give anything away. There's always a hook in the bait."

Montrose smiled. "Mister Travis, William, I appreciate your frankness, so I will be frank as well. Your reprieve from The Virus does indeed bring obligations to bear. I do believe that a cure for The Virus will be found, but not before it does considerable damage to the established order world-wide. We in America are blessed that this plague did not start here.

"Each of you holds controlling interests if not outright ownership of companies that represent the financial and industrial underpinnings of the United States economy. I believe that once The Virus is controlled, order will be restored, and with it commerce. I expect America to lead the way in that restoration.

"If you wish to remain as my guests on Delos, safe from The Virus and from the civil unrest below you, you will each sell me your holdings for the sum of one million dollars."

After a stunned silence, angry murmurs grew in a swell of protest. Montrose held up a hand for silence. "You will admit, gentlemen, that one million dollars is a princely sum, and that you can live more than comfortably on that amount for the rest of your lives. And if you like, you may remain in your positions as President, Chairman of the board of directors, or whatever title you currently hold at a fair salary. None need know."

"This is extortion," one of the men at X's table shouted.

"No, it is a simple wager," Montrose replied. "I'm willing to bet on America, that we will find a cure for The Virus, and we will bounce back, just as we have from the Depression. That is my offer, gentlemen, and to sweeten the deal, should you accept, I will allow you to bring on board one other person; wife, child, mistress, the choice is yours. Tyrell has the documents prepared for your signature."

The secretary opened the briefcase and pulled out a sheaf of papers, which he fanned in front of him. As he did, a half-dozen of Montrose's gun thugs came through the doorway and stood in a line behind the billionaire.

"I don't expect an immediate decision, but by tomorrow morning you will have to make up your minds. I hope that all of you comply."

"And what if we don't accept this deal?" Travis said angrily.

Montrose twitched his head, and one of the guards reached under Montrose's table. He pulled out a parachute and threw it into the middle of the room. It landed with a heavy thud.

"You may leave any time that suits you. Tomorrow." Montrose turned and strode out of the room with Tyrell and the guards behind him.

As soon as the door closed, angry voices erupted.

"Who the hell does he think he is?"

"How does he think he can get away with this?"

"The man is a lunatic."

Willamette stood and shouted over the uproar, "Stop it all of you.

Everyone quiet down." As the chaos subsided, Willamette took off his glasses and wiped them on the front of his shirt before replacing them on his bulbous nose. "Let's talk about this sensibly."

"Sensibly?" shouted one of the others. "You're as crazy as he is."

"Yeah," shouted another. "This is insane. I spent my whole life building my business and I'm not going to give it away."

"I agree. I'm not selling my company at any price." said a portly man in a red cable knit sweater that made him look like an apple on a stick.

Willamette raised his hands palms forward. "Listen to yourselves. Insane? The whole world is teetering on the edge of a cliff. We're watching it all slide off into destruction, and you're worried about holding onto your majority shares. Montrose, or anyone else with the cash could just wait for your stock to plummet in a month or two and buy it all up for pennies on the dollar. Besides, a million dollars, or five, or a dollar; what difference does it make if you don't survive?"

He pointed to the parachute still lying in the middle of the Sky Room floor. "Are you ready to strap one of those on and step off this flying hotel?" The murmurs fell to silence. "And when you land, back in the plague zone, then what? In a day or two you'll start oozing plague-sweat again just like all of us did before we got here. Maybe what Montrose is doing is illegal, immoral, unethical, but we can sort that out when—if The Virus is stopped. Let the Courts decide, if there are still any courts left when this is all over."

"He's right," X said, trying to defuse what was about to become a riot. "And who here doesn't have someone he wants to bring along and be saved." His gaze swept the room. "Montrose said he's gambling on America; well, so are all of us. Besides, a million dollars in cash should be enough for any of you to live like royalty for the rest of your days, and your children too, for that matter. I say let's ride it out and see what happens."

Heads began to nod around the room. The murmuring swelled again and Willamette stepped closer to X. "You made a good point, Haines," he said. "I—" Willamette winced in pain and clutched his chest. His mouth opened, but nothing came out but a choking cough. He slumped to the floor, his glasses falling from his nose. X and others lifted him into a chair. "Heart—pills in pocket."

X found the pill case in the pocket of Willamette's trousers and put one of the blue spansules under his tongue. "Montrose must have a doctor on board; get him!" X shouted, undoing Willamette's necktie. The man's breathing became labored, in and out in shuddering gasps. His skin was turning grey. "Hurry!"

"I say let's ride it out..."

Within minutes, a crewman in a white smock arrived with a medical kit, in time to pronounce Willamette dead.

X X X

Back in his cabin, X pondered his options and found few. He could call for airplanes to harry the Delos, possibly even force her to land, but what would that accomplish? All that would do is put everyone on board back in jeopardy of The Virus. His radio contact was limited at best, and this far north, he wasn't even certain his message had gotten through.

He could parachute from the dirigible, but at that altitude the cold and rarified air would likely kill him before he reached the ground. And once he did, even his survival skills and training may not be enough to keep him alive on the frozen waste below. If Montrose had created The Virus in his laboratories, he would not have loosed it on the world without a way to control it, X thought. He ground his teeth in frustration that all he could do for the moment was wait and see what happened next.

X didn't have to wait very long. Tyrell knocked at the stateroom door within an hour and said that Montrose wanted to see him. X followed the secretary up the stairs to the third level and through the Sky Room, where clusters of men still sat at the tables, heads together in hushed, earnest conversation.

"This way, sir." Tyrell opened the door to Montrose's quarters and led X inside. He stepped back and let X enter through the red leather door into the salon. The lights were off, but the room was ablaze with color from the dancing glow of the aurora borealis, painting the walls with unearthly hues and dancing shadows as the Northern Lights pulsed and swelled beyond the glass.

X stood open mouthed in spite of himself, gazing at the fantastic scenario.

"Do you think me mad?" Montrose was suddenly at X's elbow. "Please speak frankly."

"I'm reserving judgment. I would like to see what happens next."

Montrose chuckled. "Ever the clever words. I admire you your gift. I never cultivated a silver tongue. Of course, I never had any need to be anything but blunt, and I'll be blunt now. I have some things to tell you, and something to offer you."

Montrose stared through the glass at the eerie bands of color. "I am the sort of man who does nothing rashly."

"That is your reputation."

"What would you say if I told you that Montrose Research created The Virus? And that the cure was developed simultaneously before The Virus was ever released on the world?"

X's head swung sharply to look Montrose in the eye, but he said nothing.

"Are you shocked, Mister Haines?"

"If I am shocked at anything, it is your frankness at telling me."

"Hear me out. When I am finished, you will have a decision to make, and I don't mean whether to sell Consolidated Firearms."

"Aren't you afraid that I'll tell others? The authorities?"

"Once you have made your decision about what I will offer you, that will be a moot issue, one way or the other."

Meaning I'll accept or his thugs will kill me, X thought. "Go ahead. You've got me curious."

"The world has been slowly disintegrating for decades; morally, socially, economically, since World War I began. What is the prophecy? 'Nations in turmoil seeing no way out?' There's another world war brewing in Europe as we speak, and it promises to be worse than the First." Montrose snorted. "The War to End all Wars. What drivel."

X was silent.

"I have found a way to resolve the situation; simply sweep everything off the board and begin again."

"What? Go back to the Stone Age? If that's what you propose, then you are mad."

"I won't allow it to go quite so far. There is a reason why The Virus emerged first in Africa and Asia and came last to the United States. Let it bring the rest of the world to its knees, and just as America seems about to fall, the cure is found. The United States is saved first, of course, and it is preeminent in the world economy and on its political stage as well. It will take the other nations the next century to catch up, if they ever do."

"I see," X said. "But why buy out the Wall Street Thirty?"

"I mentioned preserving the intellectual seed grain for the future. You and they are the men who know how to create, invent, build, make things happen. Besides, after all the trouble, effort, and resources I've expended to make this plan work, I expect a return on my investment. Why should others benefit from my scheme when they haven't lifted a finger? But more important, the tools to refashion the world will be in my hands. I will bring the world back from the brink. The world will be a far better place when I'm done."

X looked to Montrose who stared rapt into the aurora, and saw the madness gleaming in his eyes. Yes, remake the world to your liking and rule over it with an iron fist, X thought. "And you have the cure in hand already?"

"Ready to release into the atmosphere once I have everything in place."

"I understand," X said. "The scheme is brilliant, bold, diabolical, and far from mad. But why tell me about it?"

"Because I need someone to help me. The man I chose to be my right hand is dead."

"Willamette." Suddenly X realized that in their conversations, Willamette was sounding him out, as he likely did all the others.

Montrose nodded, the colored lights dancing on his face. "Yes, Willamette. I miscalculated the state of his health. With him gone, I need another man of his acumen and presence to help me coordinate what will be the greatest plan in the history of humanity. That is what I offer you. Accept or refuse."

"I'd need to know more, much more."

"And you will, as circumstance demands it."

"You seem to have things well in hand now. Why do you even need me? Why did you need Willamette?"

"One doesn't get as far in life as I have without being realistic. What happened to Willamette could happen to me or to you or to anyone. I cannot risk the plan being derailed should my health fail or I meet with an accident."

"Sensible," X said. "One other question: why me?"

"Because while others erupted in anger and panic at my buyout proposal, you spoke logically, rationally. As Willamette tried to calm the crowd, you took his side. You have the intellect and mental stamina capable of separating issue from emotion. Accept, and the rewards will be beyond imagining; power, wealth, survival. Refuse, and as you observed earlier, it's a long way to the ground."

"You expect me to make a decision here and now?"

"The world is dying. There is no time to think about it."

X stood unmoving for a full minute before answering. He teetered between killing Montrose where he stood and buying into the devilish plan to attack it as an insider. "I accept."

"Don't think for a minute this was a snap decision, Bob," Montrose said. "I studied all of you carefully before this venture ever began. You were actually my second choice as Willamette's replacement. Billings, the meat packer was my first."

"He refused?"

"No, when I saw his reaction to my proposal before the group, I could see that he lacked the objectivity to do the job properly. I realized that you, my friend, lack nothing that I need." Montrose gestured to the leather armchairs. "Let us have a brandy and enjoy this magnificent sight."

Back in his stateroom, X tuned the radio to a news broadcast. Sixteen members of the House of Commons and five of the House of Lords had succumbed to The Virus so far. Rioting in Liverpool had half the city on fire, and the story was the same or worse in other places. The President declared martial law, and troops were dispatched to the major cities of America. If Montrose had the cure, he would have to release it quickly, or there would be no world to save.

The evening had mixed blessings. On one hand, X had learned very quickly what Montrose had done and intended to do, saving him the time and risk of finding out. On the other, Montrose's announcement had as much effect as throwing a basket of cobras into the middle of the room. All of Montrose's security thugs would be on high alert, making snooping around the Delos a dangerous pursuit.

His agreement to replace Willamette might give him more freedom to move around the ship, but his new status probably wouldn't be explained to the crew before morning. He had to sit tight and wait; something that he didn't like, but something experience had taught him to endure out of necessity.

He couldn't risk sending a message at that moment for fear that Montrose's radio operator would be on the watch after the shock of the announcement. Figuring he had better rest while he had the opportunity, X lay back on the berth and closed his eyes. He had done many solo missions in his career, but ten thousand feet in the air over an icy wasteland, seldom had he ever felt so completely alone.

X X X

The knock came a little after six. Tyrell spoke through the door. "Mister Haines? Mister Montrose would like you to join him for breakfast."

"Give me a few minutes, please."

"Yes, sir. I'll wait."

X had been awake for hours. He'd had to shave very carefully around the false chin so that an absence of stubble wouldn't give him away. A last check in the mirror assured him that his makeup and appliances were correct. He was still dressed from the night before but decided that Montrose wouldn't mind. He opened the stateroom door and found the smiling Tyrell. Beside him, Thomas stood holding the freshly pressed suit.

"The staff found this in your pocket when they pressed the coat."

X felt a chill run through him and put on his best poker face. What had he forgotten? Tyrell held out a small velvet bag. "The staff counted twenty-four diamonds, as did I. Is that correct?"

"Yes," X said. "In all of the rush I'd forgotten about them." He took the blue bag from Tyrell and slid it into his trouser pocket, stepping back to allow Thomas into the stateroom to hang his suit.

"Please follow me, sir," Tyrell said. "Thomas will lock up."

After he's searched the room, X thought. *Montrose would like to be absolutely certain of his choice. But Thomas will find nothing suspicious.*

As they passed through the Sky Room, men were scattered through the area, most eating breakfast alone. X saw Ernie Watson at one of the tables, and when he spotted Tyrell leading X to Montrose's quarters, Watson jumped from his chair. "Hey, wait a minute, Haines!" Everyone else stopped eating and talking staring as Ernie came at a fast walk. "Where are you going? No, don't bother telling me. I already know. You're on his team, aren't you? I should have known I couldn't trust you, you—"

The big man lunged forward, his hands like claws grabbing for X's face. As X stepped back, Tyrell grabbed one of Watson's arms and with a twist of his hips pulled him off balance and threw him to the floor. Watson landed with a heavy thud on his back, his eyes wide with surprise and fear. Tyrell held Watson's wrist in both hands, a foot in his armpit. "Calm yourself, Mister Watson. Please don't force me to harm you."

"You smarmy little bastard," Watson sputtered, "I'll rip off your head. I'll—" He twisted his torso, swinging at Tyrell with his free hand. He screamed as the little secretary, still smiling, expertly dislocated his shoulder. Others stood up at their tables, but quickly sat again when the waiters set down their trays and took positions around Tyrell, like trained dogs waiting for the command to attack.

"Take Mister Watson to the Infirmary," Tyrell told the waiters, and two of them lifted the moaning Watson to his feet and half carried, half dragged him from the Sky Room. Tyrell ushered X through the door and closed it behind them. "That was unfortunate, but predictable."

X found Montrose in the salon, this time with the draperies closed. A table was set for two with carafes of coffee and tea and a silver filigreed cream pitcher and sugar bowl. Montrose stood as X entered. "Good morning, Bob. Did you sleep well, or did you sleep at all?"

"Not very much, I'm afraid, Mister Montrose. I had a lot to think about."

"Please call me Elias, Bob. Coffee? Tea?"

"Coffee, please."

"Cream and sugar?" X began to shake his head. "Oh, that's right; you prefer it black." Montrose had done his homework on all of the Wall Street Thirty.

"I hope you like eggs Benedict."

"Very much," X said. He sipped the coffee. "Excellent."

"A special blend from Turkey, but I fear that once it is gone, it will be a long time before I can enjoy it again. A temporary inconvenience. Tell me, Bob, why do you still wear your wedding ring? It's been three years since Myra died."

X set the cup on the saucer and turned the ring on his finger, carefully considering his answer. "She was by my side for so long. I still think of her every day, even three years later."

Montrose frowned slightly. "I appreciate loyalty, demand it actually, but perhaps you need a distraction." He rang a small silver bell, and breakfast arrived, served by one of the most strikingly beautiful women X had ever seen. She wore a low-cut satin dress the color of sapphires, the skirt slit almost to her hip. The petite blonde set the plate before X, bending enough to give him a glimpse of her ample bosom. "This is Mister Haines, Chloe." Chloe smiled, lips parting over rows of perfect teeth. "May I bring either of you anything else, sir?"

Montrose smiled and traced a finger along her exposed thigh. "Not now, my dear, but perhaps you might bring something to Mister Haines' stateroom later."

"It would be a privilege." She smiled at the men, and left them to their breakfast.

"I have so many questions, Elias," X said.

"I would think it odd if you didn't." He set down his cup and stared across the table. "Willamette prepared for months. I'm afraid a crash course in the whole operation is in order. George will bring you the appropriate materials to study and he will brief you on all you need to know at this point. Much will depend on the cooperation of our guests."

"Do you expect much resistance?"

"Less today than last night. We are dealing with men who are accustomed to controlling their circumstance. That control has been wrenched away, and it frightens them. Offering them a choice gives them the illusion that they still control their lives. I anticipate that ninety percent will agree immediately. In fact, several have already conveyed that sentiment this morning."

"I know one who won't agree, Ernie Watson."

"Some people need more persuasion than others, and if he refuses, I'll simply send him on his way. We'll fly south and drop him off at the first town we reach in Canada, along with anyone else who refuses."

"Aren't you worried about legal repercussions?"

"For what? Buying companies for more than most are worth in the current situation and offering sanctuary and survival to their former owners? I don't think any court would prosecute me, especially after I rescue the world from The Virus. Who would dare to put the Savior of the World on trial?"

"Point taken. I hope you're right, Elias, because if it happens, I'll be standing in the dock right beside you."

Montrose raised his cup in salute and nodded his head. "In for a penny, Bob …"

X X X

Tyrell came to X's stateroom an hour later with three file folders under his arm. "These documents will brief you sufficiently to assume the role Mister Montrose wishes you to play in the operation." He set them on the desk. "He would like you to begin immediately."

"All right," X said, opening the first. He flipped through the pages and saw that it was a set of reports in order from the most recent to the least of the progress of the dissemination of The Virus. Any single page of the documents would be enough on its own to see Montrose hanged for murder, if not treason, or a dozen other crimes. "I'll begin now."

Tyrell sat in the armchair. "I'll remain here with you in case you have any questions." He wasn't fooling X. Tyrell had orders to not allow the briefing materials out of his sight, lest they fall into other hands. "Do you mind if I smoke?"

X cursed inwardly. What he wanted more than anything was five minutes alone with the documents and the microfilm camera hidden in his valise, but Tyrell had dropped anchor. "Tell me, if you're allowed, how many people have taken Montrose's offer?"

"I have twenty-one signatures so far. One or two may ultimately refuse. A few, being the hard-nosed businessmen that they are, are holding out, thinking they may get a better deal. They won't. I expect that by noon, almost all will be in the fold."

"And I assume they're not to know the grand plan?"

Tyrell laughed. "Of course not. They will be its public face, testimony to the cure's effectiveness, and to Mister Montrose's valiant role in saving humanity, hence their support of his efforts. Mister Montrose could have simply taken their companies for pennies on the dollar if he waited a little longer, but that would leave a bitter taste in the public's mouth."

Tyrell pointed to the briefing materials. "Three folders, a three-pronged plan; science and technology, asset acquisition, and public relations. People always prefer a happy ending to a sad one. Besides, what good would saving the world be if we left it in a vacuum?"

For the next three hours, X read very carefully every page of the documents, committing key details to memory. The plan was fascinating and frightening; holding humanity over the edge of destruction like Jonathan Edwards' spider dangled over flame by a thread of its own silk, then snatching it back, but only after it fully tasted the terror. In spite of himself, X had to admire the thoroughness and brilliance of the scheme and at the same time devote himself to its destruction.

He sighed and rubbed his temples. "I've read it all. I'll probably have to read it again tomorrow, because I'm sure I'll forget half of it."

Tyrell stood, his first movement since he sat in the armchair. "You'll learn more as things progress. Think of yourself as an understudy. And even if you never have to take the reins, what was it Milton wrote? 'They also serve who only stand and wait.' Elias Montrose is a giant among men, and it is a privilege for us all to serve him."

He's as crazy as Montrose, X thought.

Tyrell collected the files, tucked them under his arm, and started for the door. He paused at the threshold. "Oh, and this is for you." He held out a key that looked like the master that X had seen him use before. "You have pretty much the free run of the Delos, but I'd suggest using discretion. The crew is aware of your new status, but not our guests."

X took the key and made a show of examining it before putting it in his pocket. "Thank you."

"You will also have better quarters before too long, but for the moment, Mister Montrose would like you to keep up the pretense of your being part of the group."

The door closed and X sat alone in the stateroom, his head spinning from the knowledge he'd gained and its implications. The key was a symbol of trust, but X suspected that Montrose gave it to see what he would do with his freedom. What was it Tyrell said? Pretty much the free run of the Delos. There were some doors the key would not open, but X had never found a lock he couldn't pick.

His next move would have to be planned very carefully, and always nagging at the back of his mind was the thought that once a move was made, there was no easy escape from the Delos, perhaps no escape at all.

X X X

At lunch, X sat alone at a table. Below him, the landscape had turned from the ice of the Pole to the dark green of the Canadian North Woods. The Delos was heading south, presumably to let off any who refused Montrose's offer. The man in the red sweater took a chair beside him, a scotch and water in his hand. No surprise, thought X. The bar has probably done a brisk business since sunup.

"We've never met," said the man in the sweater. "I'm Arthur Bennett, Appalachian Mining Company." Neither extended a hand. X still wore his gloves, but conventional greetings had fallen by the wayside since The Virus erupted, plague-sweat making a handshake unpleasant. "But I know who you are—Robert Haines. I saw that business last night with Watson. What was that all about?"

X chose his words carefully, certain that what he said to the portly Bennett would be duly reported to the others. "Ernie overreacted; actually, I would say he became hysterical. I suspect that we're all on edge right now, and some can bear it better than others."

"But Montrose met with you personally."

"Let me ask you a question, Arthur, have you agreed to Montrose's proposal?"

He nodded, his chins jiggling. "Yes. Last night."

"Before or after Ernie came at me?"

"Uh, before. Why?"

"I had yet to sign. Elias Montrose called me in to persuade me. I'm sure I'm not the only one he's spoken to personally."

Bennett seemed satisfied with the answer. "And did you sign the agreement?"

X nodded. "It seemed the sensible thing to do. As the plague continues, all of our holdings diminish in value. Selling before my assets are reduced to nothing plus being guaranteed sanctuary looked like the best deal I was going to get. So, yes, I signed."

"Most of us have, as I understand," Bennett said.

"What Willamette said last night made sense to me. If this is legally untenable, it can be sorted out at some future point."

"You don't think Willamette was shilling for Montrose?"

X leveled a hard stare into Bennett's eyes. "What's important to me is the here and now, and staying alive is first on my agenda."

Bennett nodded and sat back in his chair holding his scotch in both hands and staring into the glass as if he could read his future in the amber and the ice. "I understand you're a widower," Bennett said. "I am a widower too, but I have two children, not one, daughters. How do I decide between them? That's the hell of it."

"I have no children," X said. "Neither do I have a fiancée or a mistress, or even a close friend to invite on board."

Bennett reached across the table and gripped X's wrist. "I'll give you half my million, hell, all of it if you . . . ."

X shook his head and Bennett's face fell. "There is no need for that, Arthur. You bring one of your children aboard, and I'll bring the other." Bennett gasped. "Keep the money, you'll need it and they will too, or none of us will need it at all."

Bennett's eyes filled with tears. "Thank you, thank you. God bless you."

God bless me? X thought. I'd much rather He bless my efforts, that way He'd bless us all.

After lunch, X returned to his stateroom and switched on his transmitter. Over Canada, he had a much better hope that his signal would be received. He quickly tapped out the coded message: *M has cure—pursuing*.

X knew he should break off the connection immediately before it was detected, but he waited heartbeat after heartbeat until the coded reply came through the tiny earpiece: *Received-free*.

Free, the word that authorized him to do whatever was necessary to prosecute the mission. A plan was forming in X's head, but it would require every iota of his training, skill, and nerve to make it succeed.

A knock at the door. "Who is it?" X said, fearing that his signal had been detected and that it would be Tyrell with a couple of gun thugs. "Who is it?"

The voice that answered was so soft that he almost didn't hear it through the panel of the door. "Chloe."

X opened the stateroom door. Chloe stood in the corridor. She'd changed from the sapphire gown from breakfast into a red silk sarong and halter. She didn't wait for an invitation, but rather slipped past X and into the stateroom. She smiled, her perfect teeth gleaming behind full red lips.

"Aren't you going to close the door, Mister Haines, or may I call you Bob?"

"Look, Chloe, I—" X hesitated, and Chloe pushed the door shut and threw the deadbolt.

"Elias said that you might be lonely and enjoy some company." She shrugged and her halter fell around her feet, revealing her full, perfect breasts. A push at her hips, and the sarong fell as well, revealing all her naked beauty.

She raised her arms over her head and pirouetted. "Do you like what you see, Bob?" She put her hands under her breasts and lifted them, offering them to him. Chloe put her arms around X's neck and pulled his face to hers.

X had the same emotions of any man and he felt them stir, but if he gave in to temptation, made love to Chloe, his disguise would never hold, and he would have to either kill her or let her tell Montrose that he was an impostor. Either outcome would be the failure of his mission. X made a difficult decision. He shoved her back and slapped her across the face, harder than he liked, but he had to make his point.

Chloe gasped and put a hand to a cheek that was already blooming in an angry red patch. X grabbed her by the arm and opened the stateroom door. "Get out," he snarled. He pushed her roughly into the corridor, startling two men passing through, then he threw her clothing after her and slammed the door.

He leaned against the wall, taking deep breaths and slowing his heartbeat. Now he had another problem: what he would tell Elias Montrose after Chloe made her report.

X X X

By mid-afternoon, the gossip circulating among the businessmen had it that all but two of them had signed Montrose's agreements, Ernie Watson and Timothy Brokaw, the majority shareholder in a Nevada silver mining company. No one could confirm the rumors, however, because neither Watson nor Brokaw had been seen the entire day.

In his cabin, X removed the white cotton gloves to touch up his make-up. When he picked up a brush between his thumb and forefinger, the handle no longer felt slippery. He dragged the tip of his forefinger across the white porcelain of the sink and saw no oily smudge. The plague-sweat

"Elias said that you might be lonely and enjoy some company."

was gone. He felt a wave of relief at the realization that The Virus was no longer active in him. One less contingency as he formed his plan.

By his reckoning and the compass, X determined that the Delos was maintaining a southeast heading and moving deeper into Canada. He could also see by looking out his window that the dirigible was flying much lower. The dark evergreens below stood shoulder to shoulder. Undulating in the wind, their tops gave the illusion of waves in a dark sea. Events were reaching a critical point. Soon, Watson and Brokaw would either have to agree to sell or be put on the ground.

He considered the possibility of trying to place a message with either of the men, but immediately dismissed the idea. Watson felt betrayed by the man he thought was Robert Haines, and Brokaw was an unknown factor. Further, the two had been sequestered, probably to prevent them from rallying support and causing dissension. X could see no way to speak to either of the men or to plant a physical message on either of them. He expected that the pair would be given one last chance, and that it would happen in front of the group.

X was right. A little before five o'clock, the drone of the motors stopped. Thomas came down the corridor knocking on doors to summon everyone to the Sky Room. X noticed that Thomas didn't knock on every door. The crew knew who was in his stateroom and who was not.

Upstairs in the Sky Room, the whole company was assembled at the dining tables, now in night club configuration with an empty space in the middle. Most of Montrose's crew stood at the periphery while Watson and Brokaw stood in the center of the room like schoolboys in the principal's office. Watson's arm was in a sling, but his flushed face held a fierce expression. X realized he wouldn't yield. Brokaw was more difficult to read, his face impassive.

The door opened, and Montrose strode in followed by Tyrell. He stood before the resisters for a full minute before he spoke. "You have had sufficient time to consider my offer, gentlemen. Mister Watson, have you changed your mind?"

Ernie's teeth curled back in a sneer. "You think you can just snap your fingers and make us jump like your trained apes." He glared at Tyrell, who smiled back at him. "I won't sell, and you can bet as soon as I get back to New York, the whole world is going to hear about your strong arm scheme."

"Ernie, don't—" one of the others said, but a sharp glance from Montrose cut him short.

Montrose smiled. "As I promised, I will put you safely on the ground where people will be waiting to take you home. As for telling anyone anything, feel free. I suspect the American government will get to your allegations a month or two after they finish quelling riots and burying the ever-increasing dead. And what will you tell them? That I plucked you from doom's path, made you comfortable while the altitude dissipated The Virus and offered you financial security and unlimited safety? I doubt that you would be taken seriously."

Ernie sputtered and fumed, but no words came out. Montrose turned to Brokaw. And you, Mister Brokaw; have you made your decision?"

Brokaw nodded. "Yes. I've decided that you are careless. You didn't count the spoons." He lunged at Montrose, a sharpened spoon stolen from dinner clutched in his fist. He plunged it into Montrose's shoulder just under the collarbone and drew it out for another strike, but a shot rang out, and the back of Brokaw's head burst open spattering the room behind him.

Tyrell ran forward with a smoking revolver in his hand. The guards rushed to surround Montrose, backs to the center, guns aimed outward. A voice said, "Oh my God." Someone retched violently.

Montrose stood, a dark stain spreading across the front of his shirt. "Someone throw me a napkin." He pressed the linen against his wound, stanching the blood.

"George," Montrose said to Tyrell, "Are we in position?"

"Yes, sir."

"Prepare Mister Watson for his departure." Two guards brought a parachute. Watson stood silent, beaten, as they strapped it on him and each took an elbow to escort him to the door of the balcony. Montrose led the way, opened the door, and stepped outside. The guards brought Watson through the door.

X followed, as did some of the group. The others watched through the glass. X later learned that they were given no option. Make them watch; surety of punishment was a greater deterrent to resistance than its severity.

A ripcord from Watson's chute was attached to a steel ring in the latticed railing. Tyrell pulled a lever, and a section of the fence tipped forward to form a ramp.

"This way, Mister Watson." When Watson didn't move, the guards dragged him forward. "Just like walking the plank in *Treasure Island*." Tyrell's teeth showed in a smug grin. "The difference is, you'll still be alive when you hit bottom."

Ernie stood on the ramp looking at the trees thousands of feet below. He spat at Tyrell over his shoulder. "I'll get you. I'll get all of you." Ernie defiantly stepped off the ramp and into the sky. The ripcord pulled taut, and in seconds, his chute bloomed like a red flower below them.

"I'm going to my quarters, George," Montrose said. "Please send the medic." One of the guards offered an arm to Montrose, which he ignored. He walked through the door alone and disappeared down the corridor.

Tyrell wiped his face with a handkerchief and threw it over the railing, watching it flutter downward. "Everyone back inside, please," he said. "We'll be climbing now, and the balcony will become very cold very quickly."

X X X

The mood at dinner was subdued. Most of the Wall Street Thirty had never seen a man die before, let alone so violently. Many opted to skip the meal altogether and remain in their cabins. As he was finishing his coffee, X saw Tyrell approach his table.

"How is Elias?" X said.

"Mister Montrose is in some pain, but he refuses opiates. He wishes to maintain a clear head. He would like to see you, Mister Haines. Come with me please."

"Isn't he afraid the others will notice? Put two and two together?"

"I believe that we've passed the point where that matters."

X followed Tyrell into a room he'd not seen before. Montrose's bedchamber was smaller than the salon, but at least twice the size of X's stateroom. The walls were paneled walnut hung with bright tapestries, and the massive canopied bed would have crowded out the rest of X's furniture. The room was an arrogant statement: This is my ship, and I'll use as much space as I please. In the corner, a radio console played soft music.

Montrose sat up in bed when X came in. Tyrell propped pillows behind him.

"Leave us, George." Tyrell gave a little bow and left the room. "When I said something could happen to me, I didn't expect it so quickly."

"Nor did I. I was afraid I'd have to step in and not be up to the task."

"Brokaw was unforeseen. I confess that the possibilities startled me."

"What about Watson? What if he talks?"

"It will be quite a while before he finds anyone to listen to him. Kennicook is a rather remote village, and the locals speak very little English, if any. He will be made comfortable."

"You said you'd send him home."

"And I will. Someday."

"And what is the next step? Will you release the antidote for The Virus?"

Montrose smiled. "The timing must be perfect. In another week, perhaps. I would like to find a replacement for Brokaw's silver mine first. I can drill my own oil wells, but I must have a ready source of silver if the plan is to succeed. Another week, no longer."

"Millions could die in another week."

Montrose's voice turned sharp. "And most of them would have died anyway. Don't go soft on me, Bob." He winced at a throb of pain in his shoulder. "I'm sorry. I'm not myself. You're right. We need to release the antidote as soon as possible, but I need that silver to manufacture more."

"You keep saying 'release' the antidote. Will you put it in the water? In the food supply?"

Montrose shook his head. "The antidote exists in a gaseous form. All I need to do is release it into the atmosphere and the winds will spread it across America and destroy The Virus within a few weeks. That was the original plan. To manufacture enough to spread world-wide, I need as much pure silver as I can get."

"Let me understand this." X leaned in, his brow creased with concern. "You have enough antidote to cover the U.S., but no more?"

"Of course there's more, and it will go to the highest bidder. And as more is made, more will be released, but I've already told you, America comes first."

X ground his teeth at Montrose's callousness. "One thing the briefing didn't tell me is where the antidote is located, and how to release it. You could have been killed today as easily as not, and I wouldn't have the first notion what to do."

Montrose was silent for a moment, staring at X and weighing his decision. "It's on the Delos. For the optimum dispersion, the Delos must be over the middle plains of the United States." He pushed a button on the nightstand and in a moment, Tyrell appeared. "George, please show Bob the release mechanism."

Tyrell cleared the top of the night stand and worked a catch under its surface. The top of the nightstand swung upward on a hinge revealing a grey metal box with slots and switches. "This is the release mechanism. It requires two keys to be turned simultaneously. I have one. George has one. And now you have one."

"One person can't turn two keys?"

Montrose smiled. The red button on either side of the unit must be depressed while the keys are turned. It requires two heads and four hands to make it work, no matter who turns the keys."

"And there are no other keys? No emergency release elsewhere?"

"None." Montrose grimaced as pain shot through his shoulder. "Damn it all. Like it or not, I'm going to have to take some morphine. George, please show Bob out and send for the medic."

"Yes, sir. This way please, Mister Haines."

They were almost out of the room when Montrose said, "Oh, and Bob, I understand you and Chloe didn't hit it off so well."

"I don't like blondes."

Montrose chuckled. "George, remind me next time to send a redhead."

Back in his stateroom, X ground his fist into his palm. He expected the antidote to be hidden somewhere on the ground, possibly in Montrose's Arctic base where a quick raid could seize it and turn it over to the government for distribution. On the Delos, it was inaccessible from the outside. He had one key and needed another. Maybe he could force Montrose or Tyrell at gunpoint, but neither seemed a good prospect.

His best hope was to locate the antidote, force the Delos close to the ground, and force its release. Time to think, and think hard. Suddenly, a piece of the puzzle fell into place. X knew where the antidote was stored, and he saw a way that might force its dispersion.

On the bridge, Captain Willet was at the helm. "Good evening, Mister Haines." X's presence on the bridge wasn't even questioned; apparently his new position was known and acknowledged.

"Good evening, Captain." Ahead, X saw the glow of light indicating a good-sized city on the horizon. "What city is that ahead of us?"

"Cleveland, Ohio, sir."

"Remarkable view from up here."

"Yes, sir, it is."

"Well, I won't disturb you further." X strolled away casually, hands behind his back, looking idly at dials and gauges. As he passed the chart table, he saw connecting lines drawn from southern Canada across the northern United States and ending in Chicago. X cast a quick eye to the air speed gauge. At their current rate, they should arrive in southern Illinois near dawn. Not exactly the Great Plains, he thought, but it would have to do.

X X X

To his mind, X's plan seemed almost as dangerously crazy as Montrose's scheme, but like fighting fire with fire, sometimes one must fight madness with madness. The Agency's "Free" authorized him to follow his own judgment and do whatever that entailed at whatever the cost may be.

In order to follow his plan, X needed a crewman, a machine gun, and a new face, but first he had to risk sending another message. Each time he used the transmitter, the odds of discovery rose, but some chances had to be taken.

He altered the frequency on the transmitter and tapped out a quick message: *D Chicago AM prep.* He waited long enough for the first three letters of the word "received" and shut down the channel.

X left the cabin and went to the Sky Room to find that the Wall Streeters had recovered their composure somewhat. For a few, the shock of violent death seemed to have worn off completely. Others were quiet, brooding. All were drinking.

Arthur Bennett took a chair beside X. His flushed face testified to how much scotch he'd drunk. "I see you're not wearing the gloves anymore."

X raised a palm. "The plague-sweat is gone. It didn't take long at all. The altitude cure must be working."

Bennet leaned in close and his voice sunk to a whisper. "That was an awful business with Brokaw today. I never expected anything like that."

"From whom?" X said. "Brokaw, Montrose, or Tyrell?"

"Any of them. It was hideous." Bennett shuddered at the thought.

"Each of us reacts differently to stress and threat. Brokaw and Watson are proof of that. But now we all know that Montrose is prepared for any contingency. The best thing we all can do is sit quietly and let events unfold."

"How soon do you think he'll pick up our—" Bennett struggled for a word and gave up. "My daughters?"

"Soon, I'm sure. Montrose has no reason to renege. He's kept his word so far."

"You don't think he'll back out?"

X shook his head. "No, I don't. Don't worry, Arthur. He'll honor the agreement." X finished his drink and excused himself to go back to his cabin, but instead followed the stairs downward to Deck 1. He moved aft, strolling down the corridor as if he were taking a casual walk. A door opened and a crewman stepped in his path.

"Oh, good evening, Mister Haines." He nodded and went on his way, No challenge, thought X, but I have no doubt he'll tell Tyrell the time and place he saw me. He followed the corridor to the engine room door, looked carefully over his shoulder, and put the key Tyrell had given him into the lock. He turned it and felt the tumblers move. He quickly put the key back in his pocket and walked back the way he came. One stroke in his favor.

In his stateroom, X took his valise from the closet. He took his cigar case from the bag and selected a cigar with a tiny red dot on the band. He broke it open and inside found his set of lock picks. He was lucky with the engine room door, but his key might not work on others.

A small disassembled pistol was hidden in his valise, but instead, he chose a flat, thin-bladed dagger from its hidden compartment, and slipped it into his sock. Guns could be heard, knives were silent. The dagger's edges were taped, or it would have flayed his ankle as soon as he took a step. Three needles, their tips coated with a potent narcotic, went between the layers of his belt near the buckle. A powerful bar magnet the size of his little finger went into his pocket. Anything else he needed, he would have to improvise.

X turned on the radio, found a station playing bright music, and turned the volume high. Now there was nothing to do but wait. He closed his eyes and tried to sleep, but his mind kept playing out the details of his plan. He might die, and the crew and passengers on the Delos might die as well, but the hundreds of millions he could save made the risk a moot point.

X X X

It was four a.m. ship's time when X slipped out of his stateroom. The corridor was silent except for the ever-present throb of the engines. He reckoned that the Delos would be over Lake Michigan by then, although it was too dark for him to be sure.

He opened the stateroom door and peered into the corridor. The dim baseboard night lighting would work to his advantage, making detection of his new disguise more difficult.

The crew cabins were on the inside of the ship opposite the passenger quarters. X had noted earlier that two men shared each compartment, one sleeping in it while the other worked a shift. The cabin across the hall from his own was occupied by a crewman named Tully in the daytime, and by one named Osgood at night. X had seen neither of them in waiter's garb, so they were likely full-time guards.

He rapped on the door. No response. He rapped a little harder and heard stirring inside. He knocked again and heard a muffled "All right, all right. I'm coming." The sleepy guard opened the door. "What are you—" Before he could finish his sentence, X plunged one of the narco-needles into Osgood's neck. The guard's eyes rolled back and he slumped to the floor.

X dragged him across the corridor into his own stateroom and went back to retrieve Osgood's shirt and billed cap. X's dark trousers were a close enough match. Back in his own room, X propped the unconscious man in the armchair and turned the desk lamp to shine full on his face. The nose had been broken once, and a thin scar crossed the forehead from the right eyebrow to the hairline. The eyebrows were thick, and the narrow moustache looked as if it were drawn on with an eyebrow pencil.

X pulled off the false chin and moustache that had turned him into Robert Haines and went to work becoming Osgood. In less than an hour he had finished the face. His grey hair, colored dark below the crew cap, completed the job.

X dragged the limp Osgood to the berth, turned him on his side, and pulled the covers over his head. He left the radio playing so that if someone came looking for Robert Haines, it would appear that he was asleep and couldn't hear the knocking over the radio.

He closed the stateroom door and took the magnet from his pocket. The deadbolt inside the door was brass-plated steel, and slid easily into place with the pull of the magnet. They would have to break down the door to find out that he was not in the room.

The best way to proceed is with full confidence, as if I have the absolute authority to do whatever it is I have to do, X thought. At this hour, I'm not likely to run into many people. He crept down the spiral stair to Deck 1. Behind him, he heard the indistinct conversation on the bridge. Osgood had no weapons in his cabin, which meant there was an armory in one of the compartments, but X had no time to search for it.

As he moved down the passageway toward the engine room, X saw a door open, and a man he recognized as Compton, one of the bridge crew, stepped out. He was locking the door when X came up behind him, caught him in a choke hold, and shoved him back into the room.

"If you want to breathe again, don't try anything stupid," X hissed in his ear. "Tell me, where is the armory?"

X released his grip slightly and Compton gagged before croaking, "Armory? There's no armory."

"Where do you store the weapons?" When the crewman hesitated, X renewed his hold. "Let's try again. Where are the guns?"

"This deck, port side, compartment 12," he wheezed.

X plunged a narco-needle into Compton's neck, and he slumped to the floor. X left the compartment and using the crewman's keys, locked it behind him. He followed the corridor to a connecting hallway leading him to the other side of the ship where he found compartment 12. He tried the master key he'd been given first and found that it didn't open the door. Neither did any of the keys from Compton's ring.

The lock was stubborn and took X more time than he could afford to pick it. Finally, it clicked open, and he found himself in a room that would arm a small platoon. The walls held racks of rifles, shotguns, and other firearms, including eight Thompson submachine guns, four with box magazines and four with hundred-round drums.

X took one with a drum magazine and a pair of .45 automatics. He shoved the pistols into his waistband and carrying the Thompson over his forearm, stepped back into the dimly lit corridor. X felt his ears pop, signaling a change in altitude. The Delos was descending. He had little time.

He turned the corner, and looking both ways saw two crewmen, backs to him, walking toward the bridge. "Compton's not in his cabin," one said.

"Maybe he's in the head," his companion replied.

"Well, we'd better find him soon, or Willet'll have our heads."

Both laughed at the joke and they continued toward the bridge. X turned the corner and sprinted down the long corridor to the engine room door. When he came to the parachute closet he'd seen the day before, X opened the door and hid the Thompson inside it behind the chutes.

He tried his key and felt the lock mechanism click. The door swung open, and immediately the diesel engines pounded in his ears and thumped in his chest. A guard with a carbine on a sling stood just inside the door. "Osgood, what's up?"

X leaned in to speak in the guard's ear over the engines. "Tyrell wants you at the bridge. Compton's gone missing." Over his shoulder, X saw the guard at the other end of the engine room step away from his post and disappear behind a wall of machinery.

"What? Missing?"

"That's all I know."

The guard turned and when he did, X delivered a chopping blow to the side of his neck. The guard fell to the steel decking, and X quickly slung the carbine over his shoulder. When the other guard stepped into view across the long room, X waved and as soon as the guard turned, X slid quickly down a crew ladder to the bowels of the engine room and the heart of the mechanism.

If he disabled one engine, the other would be sufficient to sustain the Delos. Instead, he chose the transfer case, the complex box full of gears and cams that distributed power from both engines to the propeller system. X found the bleeder valve to its oil pump and unscrewed the cap.

He reached into his pocket and pulled out Haines' velvet sack. X poured the diamonds into the pipe and was screwing the cap back on when a heavy hand caught him by the collar. He turned his head to see a red-faced man nearly double his size in coveralls brandishing a wrench as long as his forearm.

"What are you doing, Osgood?"

"Nothing, I—" X's explanation was interrupted by a sharp clank and a gnashing of gears. The engineer's head turned, giving X the opportunity to use the third of his needles. The man fell, but the noise got the attention of the other guard, who came running.

X crouched over the fallen man so that the guard couldn't see his face. When he got within reach, X sprang upward, driving his fist under the guard's chin. The man tumbled backward but didn't go down. He drew his pistol from its holster but before he could pull the trigger, X had a hand on it, wrestling him for possession. X slammed the guard's gun hand against a sharp steel corner and the pistol fell between the transfer case and the bulkhead.

The guard was tough and tenacious. He got his hands around X's throat and would have choked him to death if X hadn't driven his doubled fists upward between the guard's hands, forcing them apart, then bringing his fists down on the bridge of his opponent's nose.

The guard fell on his back, and his arm swept under the pump. His hand came out with the pistol. He snapped off a shot that barely missed X's head, and X drew a pistol of his own to fire back.

The guard dropped the automatic and clutched at his stomach. He curled his knees to his chest and screamed. X sprinted up the staircase and through the door. He retrieved the machine gun from the parachute closet and with his other hand grabbed one of the chutes.

X scrambled up the stairs to Deck 2 and was halfway to Deck 3 when he heard a sound he'd not heard before on the ship, the metallic blare of klaxons. Someone had sounded an alarm.

As he ran through the Sky Room, the door to Montrose's quarters opened and he and Tyrell burst into the glass walled room. "Osgood!" Montrose shouted. "What's going on?"

X shouted back, "A saboteur. He's wrecked the guidance system. We're

X poured the diamonds into the pipe...

searching the decks for him now." He didn't wait for a response. He ran behind the bar and through the dark kitchen to the stairs that would lead him above the gondola to the bag room.

X's key failed at the door to the catwalk. There was no time to pick the lock. He tore the tobacco from one of his cigars revealing a slender glass cylinder covered in cloth. He snapped the glass tube in two and shoved it into the keyhole. X turned his back and covered his face as the explosive in the tube erupted with a loud bang, blowing the lock apart. He spun the wheel and pulled the door open.

A shot rang from inside the bag room and a bullet whined off the metal frame near X's head. X dropped the chute and pulled one of the pistols from his waistband. He couldn't waste one shot from the Thompson's drum. He fired as he rolled through the door onto the catwalk. The bulging gas bags on either side allowed him no cover, but his opponent had no cover either.

X could see him in the dim light, aiming a carbine. X took aim and fired, not at the gunman, but at the balloon straining with helium beside him. The bullet ripped through the gas bag, and a gush of frigid gas sprayed the man's face, taking him by surprise and knocking him off balance. X's next shot put him out of the action for good.

He could hear footsteps pounding up the stairs from below. He grabbed the parachute and shouldered into the harness as he ran three quarters of the way down the catwalk, vaulting over the dead man.

"There he is," shouted one of the guards, raising a machine gun.

Tyrell knocked it aside. "Don't shoot, you fool. You'll hit the bags."

X saw Montrose shoulder his way through the guards at the doorway. "Hold your fire." He shouted down the catwalk, "I know you're not Osgood. Who are you?"

"You'll never know, Montrose," X said.

"What's that you've got? A parachute! What a foolish idea. You have no portal to jump through." He spread his hands. "Put down the gun. I'm a reasonable man. We can work this out. I can give you anything you want."

"Which bags hold the cure, Montrose?" X pointed the barrel of the Thompson at a pair of the bulbous sacs near the center of the frame. "I'm betting it's those two. The others are deflating and those two are as fat as ever."

Over Montrose's shoulder, X saw the barrel of a rifle, a sharpshooter taking aim. He raised the Thompson and fired, not at the men on the catwalk, but at the hundreds of bulging sacs all around him.

Slugs ripped through the rubberized cloth and the space was filled with the whistling wheeze of hundreds of gas bags pushing helium through the bullet holes.

"Shoot him!" Montrose shouted.

X dropped the machine gun and vaulted over the railing. He fell on top of one of the deflating bags. The effect was like landing on a trampoline. He bounced and rolled off the first bag and onto another. Between two of them, he could see the outer skin of the dirigible. He pulled the dagger from his sock and zipped off the tape.

"There he is!"

X dove from the gas bag and landed flat against the Delos' curving outer skin. The dagger burst through the rubberized shell, and as gravity pulled X downward, the razor edge ripped open the rigid fabric. X pushed himself through the rent in the shell and was almost clear when a pair of hands grabbed his ankles. Tyrell.

X threw himself forward and through the gap, dragging Tyrell with him, and both found themselves staring at the lake thousands of feet below. X pulled the ripcord much sooner than he wanted, hoping the jerk of the opening chute would shake the crazed killer off him, but Tyrell held on, desperate, not to save himself, but to kill his enemy.

Tyrell let go with one hand, and in the pale light of dawn, X saw the gleaming arc of an opening switchblade knife. He kicked with his free foot, catching Tyrell full in the face, but the killer would not let go. He plunged the blade into X's calf and drew it back for another try at his artery.

The automatic boomed in X's fist, and Tyrell dropped like a falling bird. X shivered in the cold. The Delos had descended, but not enough for comfort in indoor clothes. His teeth rattled like a dancing skeleton. Above him, the dirigible floated like a great storm cloud, black against the pale sky.

A flash of white. Something was falling from the Delos, no not falling, swooping. The glider. X saw it gracefully turn and come to bear, aiming right at him. Fifty meters, thirty, twenty. X yanked at the shroud lines with his left arm and twisted his legs upward like a gymnast as the sharp edge of the glider's wing almost cut him in two. As it passed, he could see Elias Montrose in the cockpit, features twisted into a rictus of fury.

The glider made a tight banking turn, and this time, X could see that Montrose was aiming high to cut his lines and drop him into the lake. At that height, X would never survive the fall. Then he heard it, the drone of engines. Two biplanes were closing on an intercept course with the glider.

Machine guns chattered, raking the fuselage. A second pass and the delicate glider spilt in two behind the wings. The front half nosed downward, and as it passed below him, X could see nothing through the cockpit glass. The inside was coated with blood.

As X drifted toward the surface of the lake, he saw boats converging. Most were Coast Guard cutters and Harbor Patrol, but a few were rescue craft. Overhead, he could see that the Delos was losing altitude, and the ships circled below like sharks waiting for the gondola to touch down on the lake.

When X hit the water, he found that Lake Michigan was cold, but not nearly as cold as the air when he left the Delos. He treaded water as he unfastened the parachute harness and kicked himself free of the shroud lines. The red silk canopy bobbed in the waves behind him like a giant jellyfish.

One of the Coast Guard cutters turned toward him but it was waved away by a smaller craft, a lean, powerful speedboat with no markings. Its sleek, black hull drew up alongside him, and a man in a leather jacket threw him a life preserver with a line attached.

The crew hauled X to the side of the boat. One of them, a hard-looking man with a weathered face and a white scar across his chin leaned over, pointing an automatic at X's head and said, "Dead men tell no tales."

X replied, barely able to speak for his shivering, "Until they're resurrected."

The boatman shoved his pistol back into its holster and took X's wrist in both his hands. With less effort than X would have expected, the sailor pulled him from the water and into the stern of the boat. X reached a hand to his face. One of his thick eyebrows was missing, but no one commented on it.

"Swing her around, McCurdy," the leader said, then to X, "Let's get you home." He threw X a blanket, and the boat took off with a roar, the chop slapping hard against the hull.

X turned in the bow to look back at the Delos. It was only thirty yards out of the water now. The upper frame maintained its shape, despite the flaccid gas bags inside it, and the great airship looked as magnificent as it had the first time X saw it.

The last glimpse he got of the Delos, the giant dirigible was bobbing on the lake on its inflatable base. But the engineers designed the base to work in tandem with helium in all the bags. The Delos was sinking. X saw men jumping from the windows of the upper decks into the cold water of the lake, and the rescue boats circling the sinking dirigible picking up the survivors.

"Let's look at that leg," the scarred man said. X looked down and saw a watery puddle of blood under his calf where Tyrell had stabbed him. The big man slit his trouser leg with a Ka-Bar and ripped the cloth open to the knee. X lay back against the gunwale, closed his eyes, and drifted into unconsciousness.

X X X

Bakewell pulled the fur-lined hood of his parka around his face and stepped out of the quonset hut into the sharp wind. Ice crystals stung his forehead and in two breaths, the hairs in his nostrils were frozen. He would be glad when his turn on the ground ended and he went up in the Delos for a week and got to thaw out. He had no exposure to The Virus on the ice cap, but the prospect of warmth, good food, good liquor, and some time with one of the hookers gave him something to look forward to.

He was headed for the laboratory building. The radio in the hut wasn't getting a signal, only static, and it was time to check in with Montrose on the Delos. He was almost at the lab when he heard a faint sound over the howl of the wind. The drone of an airplane. No supply flights were scheduled for two more days. He pulled his dark goggles down to his chin and strained his eyes through the wind-whipped snow.

The white-clad paratrooper almost knocked Bakewell off his feet when he hit the ground and rolled. Another landed behind him. Bakewell turned to run, shouting an alarm, when a bullet from a carbine caught him in the calf and he fell face down on the unyielding ice. He turned his head and saw dozens of white chutes falling from the grey clouds like milkweed and disappearing into the puffs of snow that swirled across the ice.

The Quonset hut door burst open, and two men with rifles opened fire on the invaders. Shaklee ran out firing a machine gun, not at the men on the ground, but at the ones still gliding down. One of the invasion squad raised his rifle and fired three shots that punched a neat triangle in Shaklee's chest, as a white half-track rounded the corner of the laboratory building, the .50 caliber machine gun mounted at its rear spitting fire and death.

The fight was quick and vicious. The mercenaries fought to the last man, but soon, the commandos had taken the base and were holding the technicians in the laboratory at gun point. The squad leader opened a discrete channel and hailed his commander in the airplane circling overhead. One word: *Secure.*

X X X

The next day, X sat in a plush chair in the Knickerbocker Hotel looking out the window over Chicago's Gold Coast. Someone knocked at the door, and a voice said, "Room service."

X stood and reached into the pocket of his robe, wrapping his fingers around a small automatic and thumbing off the safety. Limping from the wound in his calf, he crossed the floor and slipped the burglar chain off the door and opened it an inch from the hinge side, reaching across the panel. Through the crack between the hinges, he recognized the bellhop he'd sent out earlier. The boy held a clutch of newspapers in both hands.

X swung the door open. The bell hop stepped in and said, "I'm sorry it took so long, Mister Reynolds, but I had to go to three newsstands to find a *New York Herald*."

"That's quite all right, young man," X said, brushing a lock of white hair from his brow. He reached into the other pocket of his robe and pulled out a five-dollar bill. He eyed the boy's face. "What happened to your cheek?"

The bell hop rubbed a knuckle over a blooming bruise. "Oh, just a couple guys who got in my way." He shrugged. "This is Chicago."

X pressed the bill into the bell hop's hand. "Thank you for your trouble."

The bellhop's eyes widened at the sight of the five-spot. "Thank *you*, Mister Reynolds."

X closed the door behind the boy and took the newspapers to the armchair. The front pages of the Chicago papers all carried thick, black headlines under the masthead: Super Blimp Sinks in Lake Michigan, Delos Down, Twelve Die in Dirigible Tragedy. Something to drive headlines about The Virus below the fold for a day.

The headlines were different, but the same photo of the Delos, gondola almost completely under water, the frame collapsing above it, ran under each one of them. The Agency controlled the coverage. X held one of the papers close to his eye and squinted. The spot in the foreground where a sleek speedboat was pulling a man from the water was altered so artfully, that if he didn't know the photo was doctored, he would never have noticed the difference.

The Chicago articles were all stamped from the same die, recitations of the official version of events. No mention was made of Montrose's plot or the release of the antidote. The whole affair was reported as a "tragic accident" by the press. Montrose said the antidote would have effect in two weeks, but the Agency decided not to get the public's hopes up in case Montrose's estimate was too optimistic.

The listed dead included Elias Montrose, his personal secretary George

Tyrell, and several members of the crew. Victims among Montrose's passengers included Richard Burns of Burns and Klemmer Investment Company, Albert Claiborne, owner of National Auto Parts, and Timothy Brokaw of Consolidated Mining, Inc. Robert Haines was listed among the missing.

Betty Dale's article in the *Herald* was different. It began: "Yesterday in Chicago, a valiant effort saved countless lives as the super dirigible Delos crashed into Lake Michigan, narrowly avoiding a landing in the city that might have killed thousands of residents."

The article went on to praise the Coast Guard and Harbor Patrol for its quick response in rescuing the surviving passengers and crew members, but X understood what Betty really meant. He closed his eyes and leaned back in his chair.

It was applause enough.

He lifted the handset from the squat Stromberg-Carlson telephone on the desk. When the operator answered, he said, "I'd like to place a call to New York City."

X X X

Betty Dale sat at her desk in the *New York Herald* offices. She had been awake for nearly thirty hours, watching every story that came in on the teletype, listening to every radio report, hoping for more news from Chicago. Agent X could never tell her what his missions were, but when he asked for detailed information involving Elias Montrose, Robert Haines, and the Delos, it didn't take a detective to figure out that he was involved in the dirigible incident. Robert Haines was listed among the missing passengers of the Delos, and she feared what that might mean.

"Betty." Max Willis was leaning over her desk and said, "Betty, go get some sleep. You look terrible."

"In a little while, Max." She raised her red eyes toward him. I'm waiting for info from Chicago to do a follow-up piece."

"If anything comes in, I'll call you, okay? Go home before you pass out."

"I'll give it another hour, Max, and if nothing new comes in, I'll go home."

"Good girl."

They both knew she was lying. They both knew that if she left, Max would hijack the story as soon as something new came in on the teletype to get his byline on the front page. But that was not why Betty stayed at her desk in the *Herald* office. She was waiting for any word, any inkling, that X was at least alive.

How many times she had been in the same position, waiting, hoping, praying that he would be safe. Betty went to the back room for another cup of coffee and almost didn't hear the telephone on her desk ringing. She ran to her chair, coffee sloshing from the mug. Her hand swooped for the phone like a hawk at a field mouse.

"City Desk, Betty Dale speaking."

"Miss Dale, my name is Rupert Reynolds."

"Yes, Mister Reynolds?"

"I'm calling from Chicago." There was a long silence at the other end of the line. Betty's throat closed in anticipation of what might come next.

"I'd like to congratulate you on the *ex*-cellent article you wrote about the Delos crash." At the emphasis in the word excellent, Betty gasped.

"When I'm in New York sometime, perhaps we can meet and discuss it."

"Yes," Betty said, choking back a sob of relief. "I'd like that very much."

"It's a date, then."

"Thank you, Mister Reynolds. Thank you for calling."

"I'll be in touch." The phone went dead, and Betty put her hands in her face, weeping tears of joy. In Chicago, X hung up the phone and stared at the wall for a long time.

X X X

The cab dropped X off a block away from a warehouse that looked as if it had been through a war. In a manner of speaking, it had during Prohibition when Federal agents under the command of the illustrious Eliot Ness raided the building to destroy its cache of illegal liquor and arrest the mobsters holed up inside. The smashed doors had been replaced, as had the broken window panes, but bullet holes still pocked the wooden siding where machine gun fire had raked the facade.

Overhead, the El clattered on a nearby track carrying people to jobs, homes, normality. Humans are a resilient species, X thought. It won't take long before everything is business as usual again.

Two days had passed since the crash of the Delos. Today, X's hair and rough beard were a Nordic blonde, and he wore the denim coat and knit cap of a longshoreman. He stepped around the building to a side door and tried the handle. The door swung inward, and he entered the cavernous interior. In the grey light that filtered through the grimy window panes, X saw a table with a single chair. He sat in it and waited.

Five minutes passed, and X was about to light a cigarette when he heard the metallic voice of K-9 from a unspecified point in the dim room. "Good morning, Agent X."

"Sir."

"I commend you on your ingenuity in handling the Delos affair. I must say, however, that your report of events reads like a pulp magazine tale."

"Sometimes, reality is as bizarre as fiction, sir."

"Indeed." X heard papers shuffling and silence for a minute. "In your opinion, the so-called Wall Street Thirty were all victims of Montrose's scheme, not accomplices?"

"With the exception of Ellis Willamette, I believe that the Wall Street Thirty were nothing more than desperate men trying to save their lives. I really can't blame them. Although some might carp about the privilege of the wealthy, I think that all people, offered the same chance, would have taken it."

"You ran a great risk taking matters in hand as you did. Had you failed at any point, the result could have been catastrophic."

"Some days, you have to improvise."

An uncharacteristic chuckle crackled through the voice filter. "This time, you were lucky. The world was lucky."

"It was a very near thing, sir," X said to K-9. "I'm glad that my messages were understood."

"Once I knew that Montrose had the antidote on board and where the Delos was headed, I was prepared to force a landing and take the ship." K-9 said his voice a metallic whisper. "I'm glad that wasn't necessary. Montrose may have taken some step to destroy the antidote if he thought he was about to be captured."

"And in the harbor, how did your men know who I was, since I was disguised as a crewman?"

"They were prepared to shoot you before you hit the water, but it stood to reason that none of Montrose's men or his guests would parachute out of the Delos and leave its protection from The Virus. It had to be you, and when they saw the glider trying to cut you in half, there was no question."

"I am relieved that the antidote is in the government's hands now," X said, "but I regret that Montrose didn't live to see the gallows for all of the death and destruction he caused."

"Enough of his men are in custody to keep the hangman busy for quite a while. A team was on standby, and they seized the lab on the ice cap within an hour of the crash. The lab technicians have offered full cooperation in producing and implementing the cure."

"Aren't they afraid of prosecution?"

"We gave them a choice: cooperate with us and be international heroes or resist and be hanged for treason. They all wisely decided to cooperate."

"How soon can the antidote be released world-wide?"

"With Montrose's team, plus Century's and Capstone's working together, no more than ten days."

"And Montrose's conspiracy—will anyone ever know?"

"No, we can't afford to let anyone know how close Montrose came to taking over the world. It wouldn't be too long before some rogue nation tried a similar gambit, and maybe succeeded. I am afraid that Montrose will go down in history for his hand in curing The Virus and nothing more."

X said, "What about Robert Haines. He was listed as missing."

"Easily dismissed as an error in all the confusion."

"Has he been briefed?"

"He will be this afternoon."

"And how much will you tell him?"

"Only that his detainment served the National interest and that the President extends his gratitude. He will be told no more than what others of the Wall Street Thirty know and be sworn to secrecy concerning his role in the operation."

"Please see that he gets these." X laid the pocket watch with its bullet-encrusted fob on the table beside Haines' wedding ring. Apparently it was lucky after all. "And his diamonds—"

"They will be replaced, and Consolidated Firearms will be given preference in military contracting to compensate him for his..." K-9 paused searching for the right word. "Inconvenience. There is a war coming. I'm sure he will reap a just reward."

X sat up in the chair. "A war? Where?" X said, but no sooner had he spoken the words than he heard a door close behind the screen and he was left, once again, alone.

THE END

Getting the Delos off the Ground

Although most of the fiction I've written for Airship 27 has involved original characters, I enjoyed writing a Secret Agent X story ("The Devil in the Deep Blue Sea," in vol. 5) so much that I was happy to write another. As I developed "Island in the Sky" I realized that it was a bit too involved a plot for a short story, but not enough for a novel, so Ron Fortier and I agreed that it should be a novella.

I've been fascinated with dirigibles since my childhood, but I saw them only in pictures and films until I was 48 years old. One night I walked out of a classroom building at Duquesne University to see the Goodyear blimp floating over Pittsburgh's Three Rivers Stadium to cover a Steeler game for ABC's *Monday Night Football.* Two days later, driving past the Allegheny County Airport, I saw it tethered to the ground and appreciated how enormous it was.

When people today think dirigible stories, they think of *Black Sunday* by Thomas Harris, in which the Goodyear Blimp is used as a terrorist weapon to cause massive carnage at the Super Bowl. Another aircraft, the Albatross in Verne's *Robur the Conqueror* (filmed with Vincent Price as Robur under the title of the novel's sequel, *Master of the* World) might also come to mind. In both cases, the flying ship was a means of destruction and terror for fanatics. I decided that the Delos would play a role in a more devious scheme calculated to take over the world.

In the late 70s, I read an article in *Esquire* about new technology calculated to modernize lighter than air conveyances, including the multiple gas bags employed on the Delos. I decided that it would be a part of the Delos' design, and ultimately a linchpin of the plot. As pulpers agree, next generation technology is fair game in a story, because we all know that the military and espionage communities exhaust all potential uses of any new discovery or invention before the public is permitted to know it exists. And when money is no object, the magical becomes the obtainable.

I conceived of the plot for "Island in the Sky" more than thirty years ago, but I didn't have the opportunity to write it until now. Agent X seemed a perfect fit as the protagonist, particularly using multiple disguises, so I ran with the idea. I also tried to put a different spin on the character, delving into the psychology of living most of the time as someone else, and lacking the opportunity to have normal relationships with others.

As long as there's an Airship 27, there will be a Secret Agent X. And I say Bravo!

X X X

FRED ADAMS, JR. is the author of the Hitwolf, Six Gun Terrors, C. O. Jones, and Sam Dunne series novels for Airship 27, plus additional one-timers including *Bloody Key* and *The Eye of Quang-Chi*. His novel *Dead Man's Melody* was nominated as Pulp Novel of the Year for the 2017 Pulp Factory Awards. Fred is a retired member of the Penn State University English Department, whose chairman shudders every time he thinks about Fred's "literary slumming."

SECRET AGENT "X"

by Kaushik Karforma

Agent X stood motionless on the ledge, his back pinned to the mountain wall. More than half of his foot was jutting out into the void. He squinted, trying to see something—anything—through the sleet that had been falling steadily for the past hour, reducing the world in front of him into patches of white swirling in pitch-black. He dared not raise his hand to rub away the coating on his eyes: any sudden movement might cause him to lose footing and plunge into the chasm below. X didn't fear death, a man in his profession couldn't afford to. But he wasn't suicidal—although his present situation might indicate otherwise. And he did have an extremely well-honed survival instinct.

"Wiggle your big toe," X whispered to himself. He needed to ensure that his limbs were not frozen over. He had used an ancient Japanese technique taught at the Tenshin Shoden Katori ninjutsu *ryu* to slow down his heart and blood-flow, effectively turning him into a statue, to remain motionless on this ledge 4,000 feet up in the High Tatras in Poland. Now he needed to break the conditioning because the time for movement was drawing nigh.

X whispered the phrase to himself twice more. The invisible bonds—both physiological and psychological—that had enabled him to remain on that ledge for three-and-a-half hours started to loosen. He accelerated the process by undertaking a set of deep-breathing exercises that sent more oxygen into his blood-stream. He was still a few minutes away from regaining full strength when his phenomenal peripheral vision caught movement to his left.

Not exactly to his left but several hundred feet *down* to his left. And in this weather, even someone as skilled as Agent X would have missed it, had he not been on the lookout for it.

Light! Moving upwards.

X felt relief. The intel was correct. The freight-elevator was on its way to the Zakopane Resort.

Then: a momentary burst of panic as he realized that he might miss it because he was still semi-mobile.

X evaluated his options in under a second. If he missed the freight-elevator this time, he would have to stay here for another two hours. If he moved now, he would surely fall to his death.

X decided to move now.

He started inching to his left very slowly while letting a part of his sub-conscious unfreeze his body and mind. He knew he was taking an insane risk. But the payoff, he believed, was worth the risk.

A pebble on the ledge gave away. X found himself poised on the edge of the abyss, with one foot dangling in the air.

After what seemed like an eternity, both his feet were on solid ground again.

X moved on. Sleet continued to envelope him. Gale-force winds buffeted him. His eyes were almost wholly coated over with freezing water. His lips were chapped and throat was parched. More than once, he came close to agreeing with his body that he should give up. But his mind, his remarkable mind, won every time, albeit by the narrowest of margins.

The light of the freight-elevator was only a few feet away from the level of his feet by the time he reached the end of the ledge.

X took note of his surroundings. The ledge ended about three feet from the end of the rock-face. Beyond, after a gap, was the mountain atop which Zakopane One was situated. His destination. Across the gap, directly opposite to where he was standing, was the only means of reaching that destination undetected: a cave, part of a network of service-tunnels built into the mountain. The Polish Army, which had owned this base before the Wehrmacht invasion, had left this cave entrance open. X's scrutiny of the plans provided by the Polish government-in-exile in London had found this one weak point in an otherwise-impregnable base.

Apparently, so had the Gestapo, the German secret police. Because the cave-entrance was grilled over.

X chided himself for thinking it would be so easy. He reached inside his jacket and patted the heavy Colt Peacemaker. *It would have to do*, he thought.

And then the time for thinking and planning was over. With a loud clank-clank-clank, the freight-elevator drew level with X, then ponderously traveled upwards.

Carefully, so as not to upset his precarious perch X took out a magnetic grappling-gun from a holster slung around his torso. He aimed at the center of the floor of the elevator, adjusted for the constantly changing height and fired.

A gas-propelled magnet shaped like a cup-cake flew out of the gun carrying super-strong rope with it. With a thwack! that seemed unnaturally loud to X's ears, it hit the center of the floor and held. The rope stretched taut.

And X was off the ledge, hanging on to the gun, as the elevator slowly made its way up to the Nazi citadel.

X X X

When he was 30 feet up in the air and ascending, X set in motion the next part of his plan.

He started swinging. First in small, lazy arcs, then in increasingly long arcs, building up the momentum until the moment he was closest to the cliff containing the cave-entrance, he pressed a switch on the grappling gun, instantly releasing the rope and letting himself freefall *towards* the cave and as he fell he took out the Colt Peacemaker and started firing at the grille.

Pfftt! Pfft! Pfft! The shots, muffled by silencer, hit the grille.

X allowed himself a moment of satisfaction. His half-cocked plan had worked. He could see the grille being splintered open. He aligned his body such that his boots were facing the grille. One well-placed kick and the last remaining pieces of the grille would fall and he would be inside the—

A draught hit him in the broadside carrying him away from the cave-mouth, towards a head-on collision with the cliff-face.

X, caught unprepared, watched helplessly as the mountain loomed closer and closer.

A few second before he was turned into a paste, X fired his grappling-gun at the one remaining part of the grille. The magnet hit the grille.

X screamed a silent scream as he, hanging to the rope, went down in a wide arc towards the cliff-face below the cave-entrance. He had the presence of mind to extend his feet forward so that he hit the mountain-wall with his boots. The impact nevertheless jolted him.

A metallic groan came from above. The splintered grille was slowly giving away.

X pressed a button on the gun and the rope retracted. X shot upwards, taking out a small pick-axe from his coat pocket.

A microsecond before the grille fell away into oblivion; X reached the cave-entrance and rammed the pick-axe into the ground. He pressed the release button on the gun to retrieve the magnet and slowly hauled himself into the cave.

X X X

X did a quick recon of the cave. There was no one there. He got up and walked over to the end of tunnel. There was an iron grille, locked, at the end. X slid his hand between the bars of the grille and hefted the lock. It was a standard Yale lock. *Finally, I caught a break*, he whispered to himself.

X rummaged through his backpack and took out a pen. It looked ordinary, but it wasn't. Created by the engineeers at the Office of Naval Intelligence, the pen carried inside all sorts of gadgets invaluable to the spy out in the cold. X was about to use one such gadget.

He took out the feed that carried the ink from the reservoir to the nib. The feed had been modified to act as a skeleton key. X inserted the key into the lock. A few turns, and the door was open.

X retreated towards the mouth of the cave, placed his backpack on the ground, and took out waterproof hold alls. The next part of the operation would depend on his consummate acting prowess rather than derring-do. And everyone knew that to pull off the part, one had to have the proper costume.

A few minutes later, Sturmbannführer Willi Fromm emerged from the cave. He locked the door behind him, then walked confidently down the narrow tunnel that, Allied Intelligence claimed, led to the service doors that opened into the main stairway leading upwards to the resort.

Allied Intelligence was correct. Within a minute of exiting the cave, Fromm was climbing the stairway. As he climbed, his mind drifted back to the events that had brought him to this place, events that started six weeks ago in upstate New York.

X X X

X was wrapping up his investigation of rumors of a secret army raised by the pro-Nazi German American Bund when his boss, the mysterious K-9, asked him to go to London. X was a bit miffed; being a completist by nature, he would have preferred to see the operation coming to a conclusion. Which, in this case, meant rounding up of five members of the Bund for conspiring to act against the United States.

But K-9's cable ended with a reference to Argus, a thousand-eyed monster of Greek mythology, which meant there was an unparalleled threat that needed to be contained and nullified posthaste. And who better to tackle such a threat than Secret Agent X, Man of a Thousand Faces?

So X had quietly slipped away from the militia group that he had infiltrated under the guise of a rabid anti-Semite Ivy League drop-out, passed on all the information to the local FBI Special Agent-in-Charge, and caught the next available England-bound Yankee Clipper out of Port Washington, New York. At Southampton, he received the directions to and pass-codes to open the doors of the MI-6 office in London. After performing a thorough surveillance detection run to make sure that he wasn't being followed, X went to London by train.

Once in the British capital, X followed the instructions he had been given and before long found himself in the sprawling Sensitive Operations Center of MI-6 built *into* the Embankment.

Escorted by a Royal Marine Commando, X entered Briefing Room Blenheim. The room, like rooms of government installations the world over, was sterile and functional. A table took up most of the space; a number of wooden chairs ringed the table. An immense map of Central Europe, combining both geographical features and political boundaries, covered the far wall. Next to the map was a closed door. The Commando gestured for X to take a seat and left without a word, closing the door behind him.

The secret agent shrugged and sat down. The chair, as expected, was uncomfortable. People came to this room to make decisions, not to relax. X, who preferred to make the best of any situation, decided to use the waiting time to do a little yoga. He forced his mind to empty itself of all thoughts, while whispering a *sutra* taught to him by a monk in the Himalayas. Soon he entered the Sunlit Path, a realm of thought accessible only by the mystics of the highest mental acuity. Once there, his sense of awareness increased ten-fold. Even the slightest sound reached his ears. And that was how he could hear muffled voices in another room.

A chill went down X's spine. One of the voices belonged to—

With a soft click, the door opened and Winston Churchill, the First Lord of Admiralty, stepped through.

X shot out of the chair and saluted.

Churchill waved a hand. "Sit down, my boy, sit down. No standing-on ceremony. We don't have time for all that."

The First Lord went to the map. He jabbed a finger at a spot. "Do you know where this is, X?"

X nodded. "The Tatra Mountains, sir."

"Capital. Splendid." Churchill rubbed his hands together. "I will now let your fellow countryman take over the briefing," he said, nodding at another man who had appeared at the door.

X was astonished once more. The second man was none other than Cameron Sturges, a reclusive millionaire who served as President Roosevelt's diplomat-at-large. The fact that such a man, who was seldom *not* seen in the company of heads of state, was here, along with one of the most capable leaders Great Britain had ever produced, told X about the importance of this mission.

Sturges nodded an acknowledgement and stepped up to the map.

"Zakopane," he started, pointing at an orange circle smack-dab in the middle of the Tatras on the map. "A resort town in southern Poland. On 8th and 9th December, the Gestapo and the NKVD held a series of high-level talks here. Do you understand what this means?"

X understood well enough. The Nazis and the Soviet Union had signed a non-aggression pact a few months back. No one in Washington actually expected an alliance between two monolithic ideologies—Fascism and Communism—to work, but everyone recognized the statesmanship of Hitler and Stalin. They were both looking to neutralize each other while they were busy carving out their own empires—the Nazis in Central and Eastern Europe and the Soviets in the Far East and South America.

But what Sturges was talking about went far beyond two sworn enemies laying off each other for the time being. Two of the most ruthless and effective secret police forces in the world were collaborating. X had always considered the Gestapo to be a cabal of thugs, but had to admit that they were effective thugs. What they lacked in finesse and tradecraft, they made up with their zeal and willingness to break heads. The NKVD, headed by a man named Lavrenty Beria who had, according to reports coming out of the Soviet Union, strangled his predecessor Nikolai Yezhov to death, was a master of political repression and was shaping up to be a formidable espionage agency. Nothing good could come out of these two organizations joining forces, X was certain of that. He said as much to Sturges, and gave his reasoning when Churchill asked him to explain.

The First Lord looked at the secret agent appreciatively. "I asked K-9 for the best. He has sent me better than the best," he said. "Your thinking is absolutely correct, my boy. But you don't know the half of it. Mr. Sturges, if you please."

"What I'm about to tell you is known to only five people in the entire world. The First Lord, President Roosevelt, His Majesty the King, Col. Mayer of Polish Military Intelligence and myself," Sturges said. "Have you heard of the Musketeers?"

X had a feeling that Sturges wasn't talking about Athos, Porthos, Aramis, and D'Artagnan. He shook his head no.

"The Musketeers is a resistance spy-ring active in Poland. They've managed to insert an agent into Zakopane who's provided hints about what was discussed in those meetings. She's a stenographer. She'll give us full minutes of the meetings if we can get her out."

"And that's where I come in?" X said.

"Yes," Sturges said.

The planning began in earnest. X was provided with a wealth of information on Zakopane. It was a mountain resort built during the heydays of the Polish Second Republic by an industrialist close to the then-President Józef Piłsudski. It was built on top of a mountain, with the mountain itself hollowed out to house service chutes, maintenance areas, and living quarters for the workers. Supplies reached the resort by means of a freight-elevator that moved up and down the mountain four times a day. A cable-car service ferried guests to and from the resort.

Churchill shared with X some aerial photographs of the resort and its environs taken in reconnaissance flybys. The secret agent examined them minutely with a magnifying glass, imprinting all the details in his memory. His eyes caught a thin line running between the mountains. "What's that?" he asked.

"The monorail," Churchill replied.

Built per the plans of an engineer named Tadeusz Raczkiewicz, the monorail linked the mountain on which the resort was located—also called Zakopane—and the small village of Budachów, near the border with the German puppet-state of Slovakia. It was meant to be the test-bed for fast means of troop transportation in the event of a war. The war did come, but Polish war plans fell apart in the face of the Wehrmacht blitz-krieg and the monorail was quickly abandoned. Just as swiftly it had been appropriated by the Germans. A team of engineers and fluid-dynamicists were now at Zakopane carrying out tests on the monorail.

The rest of the meeting was about the logistics of the operation. To X's surprise, both Churchill and Sturges proved to be masters of detail, a skill he had often found lacking in the upper echelons of the government. The three of them discussed the ingress and egress points into and out of Poland. X received a crash course on the various factions active in Central Europe at the present time.

Sturgess and Churchill left after two hours, leaving X to figure out the nuts-and-bolts of the operation. He stayed in that room till dawn the next day.

Over the next six days, X traced a circuitous path into Poland. He went to Switzerland, crossed the border over to Austria, then made his way to the Protectorate of Bohemia and Moravia. From there, he slipped into the Slovak State. Once there, it was a short train and truck ride into Poland.

X X X

And now here he was, wearing the face of a member of a bunch of murderous bastards, on his way to meet a bunch of murderous bastards.

X took a deep breath and smiled grimly to himself. He went through the details of the part he had to play. Then he knocked on the double door at the end of the staircase.

A vision in red opened the door and beamed at X. "Wilkommen, mein herr," she said, extending her arm.

X felt his pulse quicken. The woman was breathtakingly beautiful. Peach-cream complexion, high cheekbones, azure eyes, golden blonde hair tied in a chignon. A strapless red gown stretched taut over a pair of large, firm breasts, only exposing a deep cleavage that promised untold pleasures to anyone lucky enough to plumb its depths.

The woman noticed X staring at her. She smiled. "Liesl Honecker."

"Willi Fromm, SS Aesir Division."

X caught a look of faint distaste in Liesl's eyes as he took hold of her arm. Then she swept him away into a scene straight out of the Habsburg court of 18th-century Vienna.

They were in an immense room at the top of the mountain. Three sides were covered in floor-to-ceiling windows, through which one could see the resort complex and beyond. The complex consisted of several buildings connected to each other. They all looked like low-rise medieval castles, complete with chimneys, gables, and turrets overlooking breathtaking vistas of the High Tatras. Snowy peaks bathed in wan moonlight stretched all the way towards the horizon. Here and there small clusters of lights—villages and hamlets—glinted. X walked over to the north-facing window to try to take a look at the monorail—intel said that the system originated from the northern side of the resort. He could see the track, but there was no train visible.

"One never gets tired of *this* view," his lovely companion said.

X nodded truthfully, then allowed himself to be led away. It wouldn't take much to arouse suspicion in this place and loitering by a window overlooking a top-secret installation was definitely suspicious. Arm-in-arm with his companion, he surveyed the room.

Gold-plated chandeliers hung from the ceiling which was covered with intricate murals depicting scenes from Polish history. Gestapo and NKVD officers milled about in the room, drinking and schmoozing. Each of them had at least one gorgeous woman on his arm, some with two, and a glass of champagne in his hand. An immense grand piano sat at the corner where a SS officer and an NKVD officer were playing Brahms and Prokofiev alternately.

Considering the poverty of the countryside he had seen while making his journey, X found the display of wealth to be obscene.

"Ah, we have a new guest in our midst." A lilting voice brought X out of his reverie. He turned to see a woman, even more beautiful than his companion, making her way towards them. She was dressed in a flowing white gown that accentuated her curves. Matching white gloves extending up to her elbows covered her arms. Locks of honey-blonde hair partially covered a heart-shaped face. All in all, the woman seemed to have walked right out of a poster of the perfect Aryan woman.

X disliked her on sight.

"*Hündin. Hure.*" X heard his companion mutter *sotto voce* as the woman neared them.

"Liesl, who's this handsome specimen you've managed to bag, hmm?" the new arrival asked. Without waiting for an answer she turned to X and flashed a smile that seemed to put the chandeliers to shame. "Allow me to introduce myself. Anna-Marie König."

X had heard of her. Reputed to be one of Himmler's mistresses, Anna-Marie König was in charge of internal security, a position that gave her authority over both the Wehrmacht, and the Abwehr, Germany's professional intelligence service. She had acted as a field-agent during the Spanish Civil War. Word was that she had killed at least 13 high-ranking Republican officers and had warmed Franco's bed.

X had to admit that Liesl's profanities were on the mark as far as this woman was concerned.

He kissed her proffered hand. "Sturmbannführer Willi Fromm, Aesir Division, fraulein."

Anna-Marie dismissed Liesl with a curt nod, took X by his arm and waded into the mass of people.

The next two hours passed quickly. X, playing his role of a decorated SS officer to the hilt, laughed and danced and drank champagne and made small talk. Anna-Marie drifted in and out of his presence, now sliding over to a general and chiding him gently for not trying the hors d'oeuvres, then moving on to someone else and complimenting him on his most recent professional success, then coming back to X again and introducing him to some other people, then sauntering over to a group of forlorn Russians and buoying them up. X noted that she spoke German and Russian equally fluently.

But that was not the only thing he noted. He knew this was a golden chance of meeting so many of the people he would be fighting against very soon. His eidetic memory was taking photographs of all those present and filing them away.

There was Helmuth Schneider, the man responsible for brainwashing children so that they could report on their parents' activities. There was Maksim Voroshilov, AKA Shoumen (The Showman), who got his moniker due to the theatrics he pulled while killing prisoners. Beria himself was a fan of his shows, as was Stalin. X also saw Reinhard Heydrich, chief of the Sicherheitdienst, Vsevolod Merkulov, the People's Commissar responsible for the NKVD, and a number of other people who were directly responsible for death and suffering at an unimagible scale.

But all of them paled in comparison to Colonel Gottfried Blaschke.

An inch shy of six-and-a-half feet, the golden-blonde haired baby-faced Blaschke, stood in the room, resplendent in pitch-black SS uniform. X noted the Knight's Cross of the Iron Cross, the highest military award in Nazi Germany, around his neck. According to Anne-Marie, who whispered his name into X's ear, the colonel was the youngest person ever to hold that rank—he was only 28 years old. *And already a Knight's Cross winner. Interesting*, thought X.

It turned out that that was far from the most interesting thing about Blaschke.

No, the most interesting thing about him was the pair of rotors affixed to a shoulder harness he was wearing. As X watched, fascinated, the colonel pressed a switch on the harness, the rotors started moving, and the man himself rose from the floor. He hovered a few feet in the air, then made his way to where X and Anne-Marie were standing. He lowered himself to the floor and kissed Anne-Marie on her cheeks. Applause ensued, followed by cries of encore, but Blaschke declined with a not-so-modest smile and turned his attention to Anne-Marie and X.

He was the commander of the Sturmfahrer, the Storm Riders, that elite group of Luftwaffe who flew around using shoulder-mounted propellers. X had heard rumors about these people; this was the first time he had met a Storm Rider in person. The secret agent made the appropriate fawning noises that Blaschke was used to hearing and easily got past his defenses. *Even the most accomplished of men are not immune to flattery*, X thought as Blaschke put an arm around his shoulders and dragged him to the nearest window.

X asked about the Knight's Cross. "Oh, the Fuhrer himself awarded me this last week for bringing down two British planes," he said. X knew better than to press for details, but recalled the incident the colonel was

The colonel pressed a switch on the harness, the rotors started moving...

referring to. Two British fighters were lost in a reconnaissance sortie over Eastern Europe in July 1939—two months before war was formally declared. The last transmission from one of the pilots spoke about some sort of flying man attacking their craft. K-9 had plans for sending X in to investigate, but the operation never took place, what with one thing or another.

Well, better late than never, X thought. *I've met the man responsible and he's confessed. Maybe not now, but justice will surely come for this war-criminal. And I shall be the one to deliver it.*

Blaschke looked at his watch. "Ah, it's time." He called out to Anne-Marie, who glided towards him, a dazzling smile on her lips. Blaschke kissed her, waved at the guests, and stepped into a terrace overlooking the valley below.

Then he flew up and away.

"Where is he going?" X asked.

"The Valhalla, the Sturmfahrer's zeppelin," Anne-Marie replied. She then clapped her hands like a schoolgirl. "Ooh, look, there it is."

X saw an immense airship emerging from behind a cloud. Its envelope was grey with an enormous red swastika emblazoned across it. The gondola was pitch-black and, at the moment, was ablaze with lights. As Blaschke neared the zeppelin, a landing platform protruded from the gondola. Blaschke landed on the platform which then retracted.

Anne-Marie clapped again. "I've seen him do this many times. But each time is special."

X shrugged. Truth be told, he was impressed. The Nazis had a potent weapon in their arsenal. Properly deployed, these troops could wreak havoc behind enemy lines, and no one would be wiser till it was too late because they were practically invisible. But he was still Willi Fromm of the redoubtable Aesir Division—which was the vanguard of the Nazi war-machine's march into Austria and Sudetenland—and he wasn't about to let a small thing like a flying man upstage him.

"That may be so, fraulein, but tell me, when it comes to demonstrating German efficiency in killing vermin," X said, pointing towards the Russians, "who would the Fuhrer rather carry out the task? A devoted servant of his from the Aesir, or a pretty boy who buzzes around like a fly?" X hoped he had been able to channel the derision and scorn befitting a Junker and card-carrying member of the Nazi party successfully.

Anne-Marie laughed. "Oh, come on, Sturmbannführer, they are our allies."

X grinned. "Allies of convenience, nothing more."

Anne-Marie grinned back, then tugged at X's sleeve. "Come, it's time for the game."

X didn't know what she meant, but played along.

Anne-Marie led him—and several other guests—to a curtained-off area of the room. A table covered in red velvet was laid out. On it were silver forks. There was a screen in front.

Anne-Marie clapped her hands and the screen parted revealing some of the most beautiful women X had ever seen in his life.

Each of them was carrying an apple.

X scanned the faces of the women. His gaze lingered on one of them for a fraction of a second more than it did on the others.

"Gentlemen," Anne-Marie began. "We present you these lovelies for your pleasure tonight. They will throw their apples in the air. To claim your woman, catch their apples with your forks."

A gaggle of excitement ran through the room.

"All right, on count of three. One. Two. Three …"

The women threw their apples. The men threw their forks.

Thwack! Thwack! The forks pierced the apples which rained down on the floor.

A steward collected the apples and arranged them on the table. Anne-Marie stepped forward and started matching the owners of the forks with the owners of the apples.

One by one, the guests, accompanied by the girls they'd been paired with, started leaving the room.

X glanced around. Apart from him, only two others were left. One was a German petty functionary whose name X hadn't quite caught. The other was Voroshilov. *I'm in august company,* X thought, smiling wryly.

"*Meine herren,*" Anna-Marie said, clapping her hands. "We have only two girls left. And there are three of you. Quite a conundrum. But I see that two of you have selected the same girl. But instead of declaring which girl will have the honor of having two of you tonight, I shall call out the fine gentleman who will be pleasured by the lovely Varvara. Herr Pabst, she's all yours."

The functionary jumped up like a toad and ran towards the girl, drooling and grinning from ear-to-ear.

"Herr Fromm, Comrade Voroshilov, you two are very fortunate. You'll have the honor of enjoying one of our most accomplished ladies tonight—the lovely, vivacious Krystyna."

God damn it, X swore.

Krystyna was the deep-cover agent X had come to rescue from Zakopane, the girl who could provide the West with crucial intelligence on the Nazi-Soviet plans. Having memorized her face from the photographs provided by MI-6, X had recognized her the moment he saw her among the pleasure-companions. He had made sure that his fork pierced her apple, hoping to get her alone and then break out of this place.

Now, all those plans had seemingly come to naught.

But X was a consummate improviser. Even as he stepped forward to claim his 'bounty' he was formulating a new plan.

Voroshilov placed one of his paws on X's shoulder. They exchanged pleasantries as they walked over to the girl.

Each grabbed an arm. One of the stewards gave them a key with the room-number embossed on it. The trio started walking towards the love-nest. They started walking towards the room, the girl sandwiched between the two men and casting furtive glances at X.

Anne-Marie called out. "Herr Sturmbannführer, a moment, if you please."

"Of course, Fraulein König," X said, turning around.

"I haven't heard from Kapitan Brock for a long time. Ever since I left Spain, in fact. Would you please convey him my regards." The way she said it, she expected X to know what the good Kapitan was. X didn't.

"Yes, of course" he said, keeping his voice bereft of any sign of nervousness.

Anne-Marie's smile lit up the whole corridor. "You would? *Danke schön, mein herr.* Well, I must be going now, have a long list of things to do tomorrow." She turned and walked away.

X stared after her for some time. Why had she mentioned this Brock person? The answer was obvious: she was baiting him. And he had no idea if he had taken the bait or not.

Either way, the game seems to be up, X thought. The Fromm persona he had concocted would not stand up to serious scrutiny. Of course, the papers he was carrying were created by MI-6's best forgers; his clothes were cut by an expatriate German who was now one of the most famous tailors on Saville Row and who served as a consultant on these matters for British Intelligence. Even the food in his stomach was authentic. And he had spent many hours imbibing the speech-patterns, gait, and idiosyncrasies of a typical SS officer shown on newsreels. But none of that was enough because Willi Fromm didn't exist in the real world. X had hoped to be able to maintain the subterfuge long enough to accomplish his mission and slip away. But now it looked like he was about to overstay his welcome.

Time to move up the timetable.

X started humming "Ein Heller und ein Batzen." When he reached the third verse, he exchanged the positions of the words Strümpfe (socks) and Stiefe (boots), intentionally singing loudly enough for the girl to hear.

The girl did. Her steps faltered for a fraction of a second when she heard the recognition code London said would be provided by the agent who would get her out Zakopane, then she regained her composure.

X was impressed at her professionalism. *At least, I won't have to worry about her,* he told himself.

They reached the room. Krystyna opened the door and lifted her foot to cross the threshold.

Voroshilov gave her a mighty push that sent her flying into the room. She hit the corner of a chair and fell on the floor. The Russian shoved X out of his way and barged into the room, grinning evilly.

Krystyna moaned. The sudden violence had stunned her. She started to get back up, felt blood flowing freely down her chin from her lips cut open when she hit the chair. Horrified, she looked up just as Voroshilov rammed into her and grabbed the front of her dress.

With a loud *rrriip!* the dress was torn off her even as she fell on the bed. She covered up in a vain attempt to retain some modesty. Still dazed, she saw the man who was apparently an Allied agent closing the door. Whatever little hope she had of surviving this night ebbed. *Men! All men are the same,* she thought, as Vassilov loomed above her.

In a final act of defiance, she kicked at the Russian but he caught her legs and started twisting them.

"I will break every bone in your body, feisty one. And take a long time to do it. Scream, you—" Voroshilov couldn't finish the sentence. Someone boxed his ears in a vice-like grip and, seemingly without effort, dragged him away from the bed and threw him head-first into a vanity mirror.

The Russian roared in pain as glass-splinters pierced his face.

Dazed and enraged beyond reason, he turned to face his attacker.

And got another shock.

The attacker was the German, Fromm.

The Russian was confused. They were supposed to be on the same side, *nyet?*

"Why?" he asked. X slapped him in reply.

For a self-styled "man's man" like Voroshilov, used to bar-room brawls and fist-fights, being slapped was demeaning. It meant that he was not being taken seriously as a threat.

X knew that. He didn't want to give this animal the satisfaction of a man-to-man fight. He didn't deserve that. No, what he deserved was having the last shred of "manliness" stripped away from him, and then a humiliating death. X meant to oblige him on both counts, as much as time allowed.

So he slapped Voroshilov again. Harder. The Russian staggered back.

X raised his hand, intending to land a third slap.

The Showman had by this time regained some of his composure. He swung his arm, intending to land a haymaker on X's chin.

He made contact—

—with air.

With a blink-and-you-miss-it subtle movement, X side-stepped the blow that would have surely incapacitated him had it landed. He caught the Russian's arm and pushed it counterclock-wise upwards to nearly 90 degrees, then swung it down again before pushing it upwards again. X's strength, coupled with the momentum, pushed through the resistance offered by the arm-joints which gave away with tiny *cr-racks!*

X released the arm which hung limply and kicked Voroshilov in the groin.

"Arrgh," the Showman bellowed in agony as the steel-tip of X's shoe crushed his testicles. X grabbed him by his hair and pushed down smashing his face against his knee. Teeth fell out.

"Not so brave now, eh, Comrade. You're so used to torturing people who can't fight back that you're helpless when someone does," X whispered in his ear.

In response, Voroshilov roared and grabbed X in a bear-hug. X glanced at his watch. He would have liked to impart a few more lessons in pain to Voroshilov but he was running out of time.

As Voroshilov started squeezing, intending to smash the American's ribs into smithereens, X moved his own head back, then, so swiftly that Voroshilov's eyes didn't follow, he rammed his forehead into the bridge of the Russian's nose shattering the bridge and driving it deep into the NKVD executioner's brain. Voroshilov died before he even realized he was dead.

"*Dasvidanya*, and good riddance, you monster," X whispered.

As the corpse slid down to the floor, X turned to Krystyna who had been watching the entire scene with rapt fascination. "Do you have anything else to wear?" he asked.

No answer.

X swore to himself. The girl was obviously scared out of her mind. He needed her to get back to her old self right now. "Hey, hey, did you hear what I said?" he said. He felt bad to be so brusque, but this was no time for commiseration.

The harshness of his voice broke through the girl's shock. She nodded dumbly.

X continued to play the heartless bastard. "What do you mean? Do you have something to replace that dress with or not?"

"N-no."

Goddamn, X swore to himself. He took off Voroshilov's greatcoat off him—the bastard won't be needing it where he's going, X thought—and offered it to the girl.

She was understandably cagey.

"Snap out of it, woman," X said, his voice a whiplash. Without a word, Krystyna put on the greatcoat.

"You have the transcripts?"

She nodded.

"Where? Show me."

The girl took off her right shoe and detached the sole. Inside, nestled in a small chamber, was a reel of microfilm. X nodded, impressed.

"Good. Now, tell me, have you—serviced—guests before?"

The girl turned beetroot-red and looked as if she was about to throw up. After a few seconds, she nodded yes.

"How long do you reckon before we will be missed?"

"The person who chooses the girl gets to spend time with her first. After that, they exchange the girls. I-I myself have—four times in one night," she said, shuddering.

X decided it was time to cut her some slack. "OK, I think we're good for an hour or so. Let's go."

"Where? We're at the summit of a mountain."

In reply, X opened the French windows. A flurry of snow borne on frigid winds entered the room. X grinned and pointed outside. "We go that way," he said, grinning.

At that moment the door crashed open with a resounding *bang!* and a squad of Gestapo men streamed into the room and surrounded X and Krystyna in a half-circle, aiming Schmeisser machine-pistols at the duo.

Anne-Marie König sauntered into the room. Gone was the high-society debutante; in her place was a devoted follower of the Third Reich, dressed in a crisp black Waffen-SS uniform, a blazing-red swastika armband prominent on her bicep; a death's-head grinning down from her cap. A riding-crop hung loosely from her hand. She kept tapping it lightly against her calf. Everything about her screamed insouciance and arrogance born from a complete confidence in the ultimate destiny of the master-race.

The Gestapo agent glanced at Voroshilov's corpse. "Ah, good work. I must thank you for ridding us of that foul presence. You've saved me a lot of work. *Danke, Herr Fromm.*"

She glared at X. "Or should I say... but indeed, what should I say? Because you're certainly not Sturmbannführer Willi Fromm of the Aesir Division. I suspected you from the moment I saw you in the arms of that cretin Liesl. But I must say, you almost convinced me. Almost, not quite. So, I decided to throw you a little bone. And like a good dog, you leapt for it."

X said nothing.

"The strong and silent type. No matter, in the end, they all talk." She turned to Krystyna. "And what about you, my dear? Who are you?"

Anne-Marie walked up to Krystyna and traced her index finger down her cheek. "I'll have an intimate conversation with you soon enough. No one but us girls." She winked. "I bet you've so much to tell me. Every little detail about Colonel Mayer, every dead-letter drop those pathetic idiots in the Musketeers use. Everything."

The girl gasped at the mention of Col. Mayer and the Musketeers. Anne-Marie chuckled, a low, throaty chuckle pregnant with promise of dark things.

X decided it was time to take control of the situation.

"There is no one named Brock, is there?" he asked.

Anne-Marie walked over to him. "Ah, he speaks at last. No, mein herr, there is most definitely a person named Brock. And he *is* from the Aesir Division, if you must know.

"Except that you could not possibly met him, unless you happen to share a cell with him in Prinz Albrechtstrasse." She licked her lips. "Which you will, soon enough."

So Kapitan Brock has done something to upset his masters. Why else would he be a prisoner in the Gestapo headquarters in Berlin? I might just be able to use this information, X thought.

"What did he do? Left a spot uncleaned on that idiot chicken farmer's boots?" he asked, referring to Himmler's previous profession.

Anne-Marie scowled. "If you must know, he was smuggling priceless art from Schönbrunn Palace to—" her scowl deepened. "Why are you laughing?"

"Why are you laughing?"

X guffawed. "You people. Racial superiority, master-race, my foot. You're just a bunch of conniving thugs and criminals. And you think you can rule for a thousand years."

"Better watch your tongue." Anne-Marie's voice was hard as flint.

"No really, look at you lot. Take yourself, for example. The only qualification you got for lording it over these men is that you sleep with Himmler."

Sh-pang! Anne-Marie's bull-whip cracked, cut through the air. Its target: X's exposed cheek.

X was prepared. He had been baiting the Gestapo woman all this time, playing her ego, waiting for her to make the slightest mistake.

A microsecond before the whip lashed his face, X caught it, twisted it around his arms and gave a mighty tug, pulling Anne-Marie into his arms. He swung her around, looped the whip over her head and tied a figure-eight knot.

"One pull and the whip will crush your windpipe. Tell your men to drop their weapons. Now!" X punctuated the last word with a slight tug that elicited a gasp from Anne-Marie.

"D-do as he says," she said. The guards complied.

X beckoned Krystyna to stand right behind him. Using Anne-Marie as a shield, the two spies made their way through the room to the French windows. Krystyna climbed out the window.

X raised his pistol and blew out the lights. Then he pulled the whip around Anne-Marie's neck, whispered *"Auf wiedersehn"* into her ear and threw her into the mass of advancing guards. As confusion spread through the room like wildfire, X escaped through the window.

X X X

The steadily falling sleet soaked X to the bones the moment he emerged from the window. He was on the gable. He could barely make out the sliding roof and the courtyard ahead. Krystyna was nowhere to be seen. He frantically searched for her, until he looked down and saw her sliding down a few feet towards his left. His eyes widened. She was headed for—Krystyna couldn't control her momentum and overshot the end of the gable.

X winced. If the girl died of a broken neck, all of this would be for nothing. Then he heard a muffled scream. He opened his eyes, and to his immense relief, there she was, hanging by her fingers.

X was about to slide down himself when he felt a pair of hands grabbing his throat from behind.

One of the guards, evidently smarter than the rest, had managed to extricate himself from the confusion in the darkened room and seen X escaping. He made a beeline for the secret agent and attempted to restrain him while shouting a warning to the rest of the posse.

He never got a chance to voice the warning.

As soon as he felt the guard's hands, X thrust his elbows backwards, hitting the man in his ribs. The blow was usually lethal but X tampered it down to the precise amount of force needed to incapacitate, not kill. The Nazi, who'd opened his mouth to scream, suddenly saw butterflies, and then blackness.

X was sliding down the gable even as the Nazi hit the floor with a *thud*!

As he slid, he saw Krystyna's fingers slowly slipping away.

Hold on, X screamed silently. He took out a knife from his pocket.

He let the gutter break his slide a second after Krystyna slipped completely.

Faster than a cobra, X reached out and grabbed her arm even as he jabbed the gable with his knife, securing purchase.

She remained hanging there, swinging in the wind, before X dragged her back on to the gutter inch by excruciating inch.

They both took quite a few rapid breaths in unison.

X analyzed the situation. No more than a few minutes had passed since they'd escaped Anne-Marie and her thugs. But by now, the Nazis would be getting a hold of the situation and they would be able to figure out in which direction they went.

As if to confirm his thoughts, shouts came from above. X looked upwards to see barrels of Schmeisser machine-pistold protruding and a helmeted head looking down.

At them!

Before the startled Nazi could vocalize a warning, X took out the knife embedded into the gable and threw it.

The knife hit the Nazi smack-dab in the middle of his forehead. He toppled out of the window and fell. As he passed X, the secret agent reached out, whisked out the knife, and before his own balance faltered jabbed it back into the gable.

The whole thing took four seconds.

In the fifth, X reached into a bag slung over his shoulders. He'd been carrying all his goodies in that bag and had been carrying it around so matter-of-factly that no one gave it a second glance. He took out the grappling gun from the bag and aimed it at the guard tower at the far edge of the courtyard.

"What are you doing?" asked Krystyna.

"Getting us out of here."

"Where to?"

"Over there," said X, pointing to a small, one-storied building set flush against the guard-tower.

"What's there?"

"Our way out," the secret agent replied, recalling the reconnaissance maps he'd memorized at the MI-6 office.

X selected a spot just below the top of the tower and let the grapple fly.

It hit the wall of the guard-tower and buried itself deep.

Shouts came from above. Then a torch-beam shone down on them.

Time to skeddale the hell outta Dodge, X thought.

"Hold me tight," he told Krystyna.

She complied.

And then they were off the roof and swinging over the courtyard towards their destination.

They were less than a quarter into the arc when the searchlight in the guard-tower ahead switched on, pinning them down in a cone of light and a klaxon began to sound.

So they'd finally recovered their senses, X thought. He had planned for this.

Without missing a beat, X took out his Peacemaker Colt and fired a single shot into the searchlight, shattering it into a thousand pieces. The light spluttered and died plunging the courtyard back into darkness.

A second searchlight came on, followed by a third.

And with those, machine-gun fire from the guards atop the tower.

But they weren't shooting at X and Krystyna. They were shooting at the rope. They must have been instructed not to shoot the spies, but to capture them alive. Since it was nigh-impossible to tear the rope with a single shot and force them to drop on the snow-covered courtyard below, they were hoping a hail of bullets would do that trick.

X knew it was a very real possibility. So he continiued to fire even as they crossed the mid-point of the arc and started to swing towards the tower. His bullets didn't hit any gunner—he didn't expect to—but they were forced to duck and one of his bullets even destroyed a second searchlight, giving them a little more cover.

A little more cover was exactly what they needed.

As they approached the guard-tower, X extended his feet out. His boots hit the wall, pushing them back, and then he swung to the left in a wide arc. The swing brought him and Krystyna directly above the roof of the one-storied building X had pointed out earlier.

He let go.

The spies crashed through the roof, the grappling gun retracting above them.

And landed on a table around which five Gestapo soldiers were sitting, playing cards.

Everyone was startled, frozen into inaction for a few precious seconds. Everyone except X.

The secret agent extended his foot and kicked the nearest Gestapo man on his shin so hard that it broke with a loud crack and as the screaming Nazi fell to his knees X pivoted on his hip, extended his feet, grabbing the man's neck in a scissors-grip, then proceeded to ram him in a counter-clockwise manner against his four companions. Before they could realize what was going on they found themselves lying on the floor.

X arched, somersaulted, and landed on his feet. He grabbed Krysytna and pulled her up and was about to move deeper into the building when his innate alarm-clock started screaming.

If he had paused to think, he would have been dead.

So, he didn't think. He surrendered himself to the base survival in-stinct, honed to a razor's edge by years of rigorous training at the hands of Tashi Lama, a master of the Moonlit Path, said to be the source from which all martial-arts were derived.

X shoved Krystyna to the ground and hit the deck himself a microsec-ond before a knife cut the hair where his neck would have been and buried itself on the far wall.

X rolled over and was getting back to his feet when a boot caught him on his chin and sent him sprawling across the floor.

X wiped the blood from the deep gash caused by the boot and saw his assailant for the first time as he got to his feet.

The man was a giant. He was of average height, but was built like a tank. His sculpted torso rippled as he advanced on X, massive fists ready to pummel his opponent as vanguard.

But X had had the measure of the man.

As the Nazi sent a haymaker his way, X parried easily and in the same motion threw a right-hook. The Nazi swatted it away as easily as he would a fly, only to realize, too late, that it was a feint. For, taking advantage of his opponent's distraction, X had jabbed his fingertips lightly into his chest.

The strike, known as Five Fingers of Death, was the most devastating among the vast repertoire of killing blows in the Moonlit Path. Knowledge of it was imparted only to the student deemed the best in a generation. X had been one such student.

The Gestapo man choked as his heart burst from the pressure that was conveyed to it through X's fingers. Blood bubbled up from his mouth. Uncomprehending, he staggered towards X, then keeled over, dead.

X walked over to the other four who were just beginning to get back to their feet and easily put them down, with a tap behind their ears.

He turned and saw Krystyna had gotten to her feet. With a wan smile at her, he made for the door at the far end of the room just as—

—the main door burst open and a phalanx of guards started entering.

X hit the ground, grabbed a machine-pistol lying on the ground and started firing.

It seemed to be a futile gesture. He would be cut down in no time.

He knew that. He was using it as a cover for his real intention which was to get a grenade hanging from the belt of his dead attacker, take off the firing pin and lob it at the Gestapo men entering the building.

He heard screams and then: **BOOM!** The grenade exploded. Shrapnel ripped through the men who were jammed in and around the door, showering bits and pieces of flesh all over the place.

Using the precious few seconds they had been given, X and Krystyna opened the door at the far end of the room, X taking the time to liberate the knife stuck into the wall, and entered the dark room beyond.

Krystyna had just closed the door when a smell assaulted X's nose. Then he heard a low growl. And then, from out of the darkness, a Doberman pinscher jumped on to the roof and rammed into X. The secret agent held up his wrists just in time: razor-sharp teeth, meant for his throat, bit into the thick mittens he was wearing on his arms. X pushed the dog away and got to his feet just in time for the beast to renew its attack.

X gave a mighty shove that threw the Doberman off him. Then before it could get back to its feet, he started whistling. A strange, ululating sound, that was too low for the human ear to hear unless one was listening for it, but perfect for the frequencies animals were comfortable with. Simultaneously, he fixed the dog with his gaze.

The dog's ferocity started dissipating. The whistle sapped its will to fight; X's gaze hypnotized it. Within a few seconds, the dog was laying on the ground, completely docile, all hints of aggression having disappeared. X bent down and tapped a spot behind its ears lightly. The dog fell on its side, unconscious. X needn't have done this last bit. But he knew that dog's masters would be incensed at it for allowing its prey to escape and would try to kill it if it were still conscious when they came upon it.

He gave a salute to the canine—it had fought well. Then he fumbled for a bit and switched on the lights.

The lights revealed that they were standing on a railway platform inside an immense cavern hacked out of the mountain. To their right was an odd-looking train. It had three compartments and an engine, but it straddled the track, instead of standing on it. The entire train was coated in white mountain-camouflage paint.

"What's that?" Krystyna asked.

"The monorail. Our way out," X replied as they sprinted towards the train.

A resounding crash rang out from beyond the door they'd just closed. The Germans seemed to be using battering rams to break it open. But, the door, which was built from reinforced steel, held firm. *But it would not withstand something heavier, such as a stick of dynamite, so we better hurry,* thought X as they leapt onto the engine-car.

The driver's console was a bewildering array of switches and levers and throttles. X scanned through them, his hyper-analytical brain quickly segregating them by possible uses, trying to discern patterns, the method behind the madness.

After some time, he thought he had it figured out.

X got busy with the console. He turned knobs, pulled down throttles, adjusted levers, flicked switches. Slowly, the train thrummed to life.

X turned a wheel and the train started to move. Very, very slowly.

BANG! The door to the station blew apart and Nazi guards poured into the platform and started firing.

BRAKABAKABAKA! Machine-guns roared. Bullets hit the cars, breaking glass, chewing up upholstery, shattering the lights into ten thousand pieces.

X and Krystyna hit the floor as a hail of bullets passed above them. *So they're not trying to take anyone alive now,* X reflected, noticing the savagery of the attack. He took out his gun and fired a few shots, sight unseen, through the broken window, then retreated back to relative safety as soon as that resulted in more firing.

And then the train stopped.

The guards kept up their firing and neared the train.

Frantically, X searched for a means to get the damn thing moving again. His eyes fell on a glass-box that encased an oversized switch. Something was written in Polish on the case. Seeing no other option, he raised his gun and fired.

The train shot forward so fast that X and Krytyna went flying backwards unable to keep their balance. X hit the rear-door of the train which flung open—

—into empty air

—dropping X out of the train.

At the last second before he hit the monorail track, X bent his body the tiniest bit and grabbed the door-handle. The door, thanks to his added weight and the speed of the moving train swung wide open leaving him exposed for target-practice by the trigger-happy Nazis crowding the platform.

X caught a glimpse of the compartments that had been detached from the engine when he shot that switch. Then he saw the Nazis raising their guns, looking to perforate him as long as he was in the target range.

And then the door swung again and he was flung back inside the engine-car even as bullets hit the other side of the door. Before the door opened again, X grabbed Krystyna's proffered hand and jumped back onto the floor and let out a pent-up breath. "Whoa!"

And then they started laughing. They laughed so hard that tears came to their eyes, as the unrelenting tension of the past 45 minutes slowly dissipated, while the train made its way along the serpentine tracks towards Budachów.

X X X

Anne-Marie König watched the speeding monorail disappear around the curve in the mountains from the top of the guard-tower. Around her lay the splinters of glass from the destroyed searchlights. Her face, beautiful but cold even in repose, now glowed with a predatory sheen. This was the first time in her career that she had been humiliated so thoroughly.

X had lied when he told her that he would break her neck. He could never do that to an unarmed—or disarmed, in this case—woman, no matter how dire the circumstances were. What he had done was to tie her up using the whip as a "capture-rope" or *torinawa* in Japanese, using techniques from the ancient Japanese martial-art of restraining using cord called Hojōjutsu. The ties had been so expertly done that it had taken her men several minutes to get her free. Those extra minutes were what led to the successful escape of the two agents.

No matter, she thought. *They would soon be captured and then I would subject them, especially the male, to the most fiendish tortures I could come up with.*

One of her flunkies approached her with a field radio-telephone.

With a crooked smile on her lips, Anne-Marie picked up the phone.

After a few seconds, Gottfied Blaschke's voice came on the line. Once they'd established each other's bona fides, Anne-Marie quickly apprised him of the situation.

After a moment of silence, Blaschke said, "What do you want me to do, fraulein?"

Anne-Marie ground her teeth. She could picture the idiot with a smug smile on his face. He knew exactly what Anne-Marie wanted him to do, but wanted her to say, just so he could rub some salt on to her wounded pride. She recalled what "Fromm" had said about Blaschke—"a pretty boy who buzzes like a fly."

Well, the bastard wasn't quite far off the mark, Anne-Marie thought. She would like very much to eliminate Blaschke but he was currently the man of the hour. He had been to Berchtesgaden, Hitler's private retreat in the Bavarian Alps. He had listened to Parsifal seated in the private box of the Nazi party elite at Bayreuth. He was also a valued consultant on the super-secret preliminary plans for the invasion of the USSR which were being drawn up by the Oberkommando des Heeres. No, the man was untouchable, and thanks to the present situation, Anne-Marie was about to provide him the opportunity to increase his stature even more.

Ah well, she mused recalling an English idiom, *the bigger they are, the harder they fall.* Herr Blaschke would fall, she would see to it, she promised herself.

Smiling grimly, Anne-Marie said, "I want you to capture these two spies, Colonel. Preferably alive, but even dead would do."

"I don't know..." Blaschke was hesitant.

"Please colonel. I will owe you."

After stretching the silence to the breaking point, Blaschke agreed.

"Splendid, colonel. I will send you whatever I—"

"Don't bother fraulein. I'm sure my men and I can manage to capture two spies who are the only passengers on a train. Now you just relax, I will bring them both to you in no time."

The insufferable swine's condescending tone sent Anne-Marie's blood boiling. She curled her fingers into a fist and squeezed, imagining Blaschke's head between them.

"I want you to capture these two spies, Colonel."

"*Danke schön,* Herr Colonel."

"Glad to help, fraulein. Blaschke over and out."

X X X

Within two minutes of ending the conversation with Anne-Marie König, Gottfried Blaschke called a meeting of his most accomplished Storm Riders. Among them was Joachim Wagner, the man who'd tracked a Jew scientist through the air for thirty miles in Mexico City during the Day of the Dead festivals, then dropped down on him in a alleyway, and slit his throat.

There was Gustav Just, a sniper who could blow off a gnat's testicle at 500 feet, a man of infinite patience who earned the moniker *diablo con alas*—devil with wings—plying his deadly trade in Spain. There was Boris Schmidt, an absolute genius with explosives.

Finally there was Blaschke himself. He knew his youth and unconventional take on modern warfare frequently rubbed the more hidebound elements in the German establishment but his unswerving faith in his own destiny to play a crucial role in the formative years of the Thousand Year Reich, his leadership acumen, and his willingness to be as ruthless as the situation called for always saw him through the most brutal of internecine politics. Coming from an impoverished background—his family had lost all its wealth in the Weimar hyper-inflation—he had steadily climbed the ranks of the Luftwaffe, before catching the eye of Reichsmarshall Herman Göring.

Göring sent him to China for secret negotiations with the Black Dragon Tong, a secret society led by the criminal mastermind known as Professor Li Yin. Blaschke's time in China was very fruitful. Not only did the relationship between the Gestapo and the Black Dragons deepen, he also got trained in a number of esoteric martial arts, finding his forte in the Flying Guillotine, a particularly nasty ranged weapon used to decapitate its targets from a distance. He also found a mentor of sorts in Prof. Li Yin. It was during discussions with him that he got the idea of the Storm Riders.

Upon his return to Germany, he pitched the idea of creating a force of mobile flying commando column to Göring. Thanks to Göring's patronage he was able to overcome stiff opposition from the likes of Albert Kesselring and Hugo Sperrle. At Göring's suggestion, Hitler had attached a small contingent of Storm Riders to the Condor Legion in Spain on a probationary basis. Nominally under the command of Sperrle, Blaschke soon devised elaborate deceptions to keep his superior in the dark about his activities which included flying deep into Republic territory and capturing and summarily executing high-ranking officers. His men slit their targets' throats and flew away, leaving their bodies to be discovered by superstitious peasants who spread rumors of evil spirits. His tactics did a lot to break Republican morale during the latter days of the Civil War.

But the last few months since the end of the conflict in Spain in 1939 had been unusually quiet for Blaschke. He had been sent to Poland to "provide support" to the Wehrmacht and the SS. Which didn't make an iota of sense as his unit was not trained to support, it was trained to kill. His friends in the Luftwaffe had told him that Göring had other priorities, namely jockeying for more power while outsmarting the other jackals who made up the Nazi elite and trying not to lose the favor of the notoriously mercurial Führer.

And so he had been forced to play the part assigned to him, reducing his life's work to a mere show for the amusement of the idiots of the Gestapo and the savages of the NKVD.

As soon as Anne-Marie König had called to seek his assistance in capturing two spies, Blashcke had recognized this opportunity for what it truly was—a chance to break out of the prison he had been placed in, a chance to show the decision-makers in Berlin how effective a unit like his could be to solve non-standard problems like the one in hand, and return to the frontlines of the war with honor.

I won't fail. I owe my men that much, he told himself as he sat down in a conference room aboard the zeppelin that served as his mobile base.

Half-an-hour later, the meeting concluded, Blaschke gave new instructions to the commandant of the zeppelin. Within a few minutes, four Storm Riders—Wagner, Just, Schmidt, and Blaschke himself—were airborne, heading towards the monorail.

X X X

"Who are you?" Krytyna asked X

They'd been on the train for an hour. The monorail was moving towards Budachów at a good speed, needing little navigation on X's part. Even so, the secret agent was perched on the driver's seat, his hands on the throttle, his eyes darting all over incessantly, as if he was waiting for something to happen.

Krystyna repeated her question when she didn't receive a reply the first time around.

This time, X answered: "I'm the one in the same boat as you, so to speak, working with you so that we can both get out of this mess alive and reasonably healthy."

"Yeah, of course, but apart from that? Tell me about yourself."

"Not much to tell."

"Or maybe not much you can tell."

"Maybe."

Silence for a while. Then Krystyna said: "Look, we're cooped up here for God knows how long. Might as well talk."

No answer.

"At least tell me your name."

A sigh. Then: "Call me X."

"That's not a name!"

"It'll have to do."

"So, they've given you a letter and taken away your name."

X stood perfectly still. Only a red vein on his forehead pulsated.

Krystyna feared that she'd gone too far. "I-I'm sorry, I didn't mean it that way."

X took a deep breath. "No, it's all right. You're right, after a fashion. In this business, one changes identities so many times; it's tough to keep track of who one truly is."

You can call me Aloysius."

"Aloysius?"

"Yes. Aloysius James Martin. A.J. Martin."

"Great," Krystyna clapped her hands together. "See, now we're making progress. So, Mr. Martin," she said, casting an eye on him appreciatively, "anybody waiting for you back home? Wherever home is."

X wondered what Betty Dale might be doing this very moment. The last time he saw her, she was researching a bizarre cult in Arkansas. X knew Betty loved him, but he also knew married life wasn't for him—not when his beloved United States was beset with enemies both within and without.

"Yes, but it won't ever come to pass," he told Krystyna.

"Why not?"

X opened his mouth to speak, when from the corner of his eye, he saw—

No! X lunged towards Krystyna, shouting "Take cover." He grabbed her leg and gave a vicious pull which caused her to fall flat on the floor a microsecond before a bullet whizzed passed the space where her head had been and buried itself in the emergency door on the opposite side.

X and Krystyna rolled over to the relative safety of a corner not in direct line of sight to the window.

"Who's shooting at us?" Krystyna asked, her voice cracking in the tension.

"He is," X said and pointed to the man with a sniper rifle flying parallel to the train. "He's going to make a second attempt at finishing the job."

"Let's help him." X got to a half-crouch and started to sneak past the window as a dumb-founded Krystyna stared at him.

The sniper spotted X easily. He turned in the air so that he was facing the engine-car, aimed and squeezed the trigger. X made a few turns, too subtle to be detected by the sniper that made it look that the bullet pierced his flesh when in reality it tore off his collar and barely grazed him. Then, for added verisimilitude, he cried out once, loudly, then rolled over and played possum.

Gustav Just couldn't believe his luck. He'd studied whatever information Blaschke had been able to amass about the two spies' escape. From that, it seemed that the two, especially the man, seemed to be an exceptional operative. Well, who's *exceptional* now, eh? He adjusted the settings of his rotors and drifted closer, to get a good look at the dead man and also to find the girl.

He peered through the window. The girl was there, her back to the wall, scared out of her mind. Just waved a hand at her. The man was lying on his back. But—

Just frowned. Where was the blood? The angle he had fired in, the bullet had gone through his ribs. There should have been a pool of blood underneath the corpse. But there was nary a drop of blood anywhere.

Just didn't have any more time to think because the "corpse" opened its eyes, whipped out a gun, and put a bullet through his forehead.

As the dead man dropped like a stone, X ran to the controls, after tossing his gun to Krystyna. "Keep an eye out," he said. "This isn't over yet."

Joachim Wagner, hovering a few hundred feet up in the air above the monorail, was astonished. One minute, Just seemed to have killed the man, the next minute he was gone. Well, he wouldn't make the mistake his late colleague had made. He wouldn't underestimate these spies.

Wagner cut the engines of his rotors and glided down to the monorail's roof. Cat-footed, he ran to the center of the car, took out a device much like a medical stethoscope in appearance, and affixed it to the roof. The device allowed him to listen for the breathing of the people in the rail-car, thus pin-pointing their location: one of them was at the front of the car, most likely at the controls; the other one was on the other side. Wagner frowned: he would have liked both of them bunched closely so that he could take them out at one go, but he was an experienced assassin; he knew how to work within limitations. He thought for a few seconds, formulated a plan. He switched off the rotors, then folded them on to his shoulder harness. Nodding happily, he ran towards the edge of the roof and launched himself in the air.

X was studying a map of the route hanging on the wall in front of the control console when he felt danger approaching. He turned towards the window just as a pair of boots came through and caught him squarely on his face. Thrown back, X hit the wall with his head with great force. He saw stars for a while; then, through a haze, he saw a—Storm Rider, it had to be a Storm Rider—drag him towards the window.

Krystyna lunged forward, intending to throttle the attacker. She knew she wouldn't be able to do much, but at least she could slow him down till X came to.

She was wrong.

The Nazi shook her off his back, grabbed a fistful of her hair, and threw her unceremoniously to one corner. "Don't worry, I'll come back for you," he said, then resumed dragging X towards the door. Wagner had decided that he was going to kill the spy. He had been given orders to capture him alive if possible, with emphasis given on 'if possible'. He wanted to make it possible, but Just's death filled him with a burning desire for revenge. He knew that Blaschke would back him at the military tribunal—the colonel always sided with his men. He would not kill the girl himself; he would have her delivered to Anne-Marie König. From what he had heard about her, delivering the girl to her would be tantamount to sentencing her to death, anyway.

Wagner reached the door, opened it with one hand, dragged X to the threshold, and with one swift kick to his ribs, sent him flying out of the train.

A second later, much to his surprise, he too was tumbling through the air.

Wagner looked down. His eyes widened. The spy, who he thought he had rendered unconscious, was gripping his left ankle. It was thanks to him that he was now airborne, free-falling to the bottom of a ravine hundreds of feet below.

Well, no matter, two can play the same game, Wagner thought. He flicked a switch, and the rotors resting on his shoulder-blades spurring to life. Meanwhile, he hit the fingers that had a vice-grip on ankles repeatedly with his right foot.

X grimaced in pain as the Nazi's heavy boots assaulted him. He saw blood flowing freely from his fingers. But he was less concerned about the pain and the blood than he was about the slickness around his fingers that would cause his hands to slip.

Another kick. Followed by yet another.

X knew he couldn't keep up much longer. Already three of his fingers had slid off the Nazi's ankle.

And then the Nazi's boot hit him in the forehead opening a deep gash. Blood poured out, running down X's eyes slowly pasting them shut.

And then he was falling.

Wagner pulled up, changed directions, and started flying towards the rail-car.

Something hit his shoulders from behind. Before he could figure out what was happening, he realized, to his horror, that the rotors had stopped moving. Then he was dropping fast until—

—a hand grabbed him by his belt.

But whatever hope he had of emerging alive from this was soon quashed as he felt the hands take off his shoulder-harness. Then the hold was released.

Wagner screamed all the way down.

His body being tossed and turned by the strong winds, Agent X struggled to put on the rotors. He had almost given up hope of survival when a desperate idea came to him. He took out his grappling gun, aimed at the switch on the Nazi's shoulder that he had earlier seen him flipping and squeezed the trigger. The grapple hit the switch, shutting down the rotor, and caused the Storm Rider to fall which allowed Agent X to live for a while longer.

He fumbled for a bit with the rotors, then got the hang of it. Within a minute he was rising towards the monorail.

So intent was X on reaching the monorail car that he failed to notice two silhouettes hovering behind the cover of a crag that loomed over the rail line. Blaschke and Schmidt had watched the whole episode—Wagner's attempt to kill X and his subsequent demise. For the first time in a long time, Blaschke felt unsure about his ability to execute a mission. But just as quickly, he got rid of those doubts. He'd never failed a mission yet and he wouldn't start now. He had thought that the spy would be an easy mark. Now that he had seen him in action, he would not make that mistake again.

Blaschke made a series of complex hand-signals that gave Schmidt his orders. The explosives expert nodded acknowledgement and set off for his destination while Blaschke headed straight for the roof of the monorail car.

Krystyna had caught part of the struggle between X and Wagner from the window. She had seen her rescuer apparently falling to his death. Thinking all hope was lost, she resolved to kill herself but not before killing her would-be captor.

Krytyna heard fumbling at the door. The Nazi was trying to enter. She took a deep breath, then ran across, pulled the door open and collided with the man, her fingers clawing at the rotor-harness. Her idea was to throw the Nazi and herself off the train, after depriving him of the ability to fly.

She would have succeeded, except that X caught her wrists and said, "Easy, easy." At the sound of X's voice, she collapsed in relief. "Oh Aloysius, I thought—I thought—" Her voice trailed away and she started sobbing.

"Yeah, I thought so too," X said, giving her a tired smile. "Now, where are we?" He started walking over to the console when he thought he heard something. His preternatural survival instinct kicked into high gear. Without a second thought, he grabbed Krystyna and threw the both of them to one corner of the car just as bullets peppered the middle of the car where they'd stood a second before.

X whipped out his pistol and let loose a volley of shots at the general direction of the shooter. He heard a muffled cry and a *clang! I think I've managed to hit the bastard and make him drop his gun*, X thought.

He pulled up his pants to reveal a chamois-leather scabbard strapped around his shin. The scabbard contained a razor-sharp knife with a serrated edge. He unsheathed the knife, placed it between his teeth, opened the door and started to climb to the roof.

Blaschke, still stunned by the fact that the spy had managed to shoot his gun from out of his hand and nicked him in the process, saw his target struggling to reach the roof. Blood flowing down his hands, the Nazi colonel lurched to his feet and headed towards the edge.

After the fracas with the Nazi who threw him off the train, X had been prepared. So, just as Blaschke was about to land his heavy boot on X's hands, the secret agent pushed with all his might and the German staggered back.

Blaschke quickly recovered and renewed his attack. He tried to land a haymaker on X who caught it in the palm of his hand. That absorbed the blow but it hurt like hell. X bit his lip, cupped the fist in his palm and pushed Blaschke back strongly enough to give himself enough time to climb to the roof.

Blaschke charged, intending to catch X off-balance as he was finding his footing on the fast-moving train. X side-stepped him easily. He intended to let the Nazi's momentum carry him over the edge, but no such luck. Blaschke, who had anticipated X's move, pivoted and delivered a roundhouse kick to X's solar-plexus.

X staggered back, all breath escaping him in a loud *whoosh!* The knife fell from his mouth and landed on the roof.

Blaschke grinned. He reached behind and withdrew something from a scabbard slung across his back. It was a weapon comprising a large metal ball attached to a chain. The lower half of the ball was hollow and ringed on the inside by a wicked-looking blade.

X's eyes widened in surprise. He didn't expect to see a Flying Guillotine on top of a train in Poland of all places. An extremely dangerous weapon, the Guillotine was so named because of the way it worked: the attacker threw the ball over the victim's head and ball would then snap shut causing the blades inside to take off the victim's head.

He remembered that his teacher Tashi Lama was quite dismissive of the Guillotine. But the Lama could afford to be dismissive. He was the supreme teacher of the original martial art and could probably defeat even a weapon as monstrous as the Guillotine in two seconds flat, while sleeping. Whereas he—

Blaschke swung the Guillotine thrice, so fast that X could barely follow the trajectory, then threw it towards the secret agent.

Sh-sh-sh! The Guillotine cut through the air and neared X at incredible speed. At the last second, X dived to one side and the deadly ball passed within an inch of him. X's target was the knife he had espied lying on the roof.

But just as he was about to grab the knife, Blaschke twirled the Guillotine again and it swept away the knife.

And X was left unarmed, in a fight to the death against a highly proficient killer wielding one of the most lethal weapons ever designed.

X got up slowly. Blaschke was grinning. It was a mocking grin, a grin of supreme confidence in the outcome, a grin that said that no matter what he tried, X was doomed.

X kept his face impassive but inside he was smiling too. His opponent was too confident and that would bring him down.

Blaschke was tired of this game. He wanted to kill this agent, get the girl back to Zakopane, and go back to his airship. He swung the Guillotine again.

X arched his body almost parallel to the roof and let the ball pass over him. In the same motion, he grabbed the chain and pulled Blaschke towards him. The Nazi had anticipated the ploy and stood his ground.

Which was okay by X because the pulling was only a feint to mask his real maneuver which was—

—using the weapon's momentum to swing it back towards Blaschke.

As the ball whipped towards the Storm Riders commander, X dropped to the roof and slid towards Blaschke. Preoccupied with the incoming Guillotine, Blaschke did not notice the secret agent until he was directly beneath hum.

X jack-knifed his body, caught Blaschke's throat and shoved it into the maw of the Flying Guillotine which snapped shut.

Ka-chunk!

The maw opened and Blaschke's head dropped out, rolled over to the edge of the roof and fell. His torso remained standing for a second, then toppled sideways.

X let out a breath and turned around.

They were nearing a river on the far side of which, the lights of Budachów could be seen. Ahead was a suspension bridge through which the monorail track passed.

X frowned. Something was lying on the track right on the center of the track on the bridge. And then he heard Krystyna's scream, looked down, and saw her being flown away by a Storm Rider. The bastard turned, gave him a mocking salute and resumed his flight.

The train entered the bridge. It was a few seconds away from the thing lying on the tracks, which, X was certain, was a mine.

X grabbed a gun he had seen Blaschke was carrying, thrust it into his jacket pocket, picked up the Guillotine, swung it like Blaschke did and threw it towards the main suspension cable. The chain whipped itself around the cable, and weighed down by the ball, became taut. Grabbing the other end of the chain, X leapt off the roof of the monorail car just as it hit the mine.

BOOM! As the night sky lit up, X swung out in a long, low arc, headed for Krystyna. The Nazi, hearing the explosion, turned around, saw X coming towards him, his extended right hand carrying a gun.

That was the last thing he ever saw. X opened fire. Two shots hit Boris Schmidt squarely in his face, mashing it into unrecognizable pulp. He died before he could even scream. His hand released Krystyna who started falling.

At the lowermost point of the arc, X let go of the chain, dropped in free-fall, grabbed Krystyna, then emptied the gun into the river below. He needed to disturb the water so that it wouldn't feel like concrete when they hit it.

The water rippled.

X and Krystyna hit the river with a splash.

X X X

Two hours later, the duo made their way through a forest to the Budachów bus-station where X snuck into the storage lockers and raided a cache put there by the Musketeer network on his instructions. The cache contained fake identities and clothes for himself and the girl.

They made their way into the Slovak State, where they were met by sympathizers to the Czech government-in-exile. They spirited them away to London.

THE END

CONGRESS OF EVIL

Adolf Hitler and Josef Stalin were consummate survivors. Having reached the pinnacle of their respective country's political power-structures through guile, cunning, and ruthlessness, both were prepared to do absolutely anything to cling to the top—including forging alliances with each other despite being mortal enemies.

In 1939, they entered into a non-aggression pact. Ostensibly, the pact was supposed to guarantee that neither side would attack the other and paved the way for economic treaties that gave the Nazis access to foodstuff and vital raw materials from the USSR, and the Soviets' naval guns, air-craft, and plans for the battle-ship *Bismarck*.

Note the word "ostensibly" in the previous paragraph.

In reality, there were secret protocols to the pact. These protocols divided Eastern and Central Europe into spheres of influence between the two powers anticipating territorial and political rearrangements—euphemism for the German invasion of Poland on September 17, 1939, and the Soviet invasion of Poland that followed a day later.

It's in the context of this division of hitherto-sovereign lands by two rapacious powers engaged in an alliance of convenience that the Gestapo-NKVD conferences—one of which takes place in Zakopane and forms the background of the story you've just read—must be viewed.

Officials of the Gestapo met their NKVD counterparts for the first time in October 1939 in Lwów, Poland. The agenda was to decide what to do with the civilians while their homeland was being partitioned.

The series of meetings that followed the October one included the Zakopane conference where a diabolical plot was hatched. It's goal: the complete and utter destruction of the Polish intelligentsia. On 20th February 1940, Adolf Eichmann, representing Germany, and Grigory Litvinov, representing the USSR, met at Zakopane to thrash out the de-tails of the AB-Aktion and the Katyn Forest Massacre, which resulted in the liquidation of Polish upper-class intellectuals and the officer corps, thereby removing the possibility of rebellion.

When I approached Ron about the possibility of writing for Airship 27, he assigned me Secret Agent X. I read up on the character—the bible and the stories in the Airship 27 anthologies already published—and, for the life of me, couldn't get a handle on a story. Whenever I felt I had an idea worth exploring, it seemed to evaporate.

After some thought, I realized that the ideas I had had up to that point—the Spanish Civil War, fifth-columns, even an X-version of Die Hard set in the Statue of Liberty—weren't working because they lacked that…punch, that spark, that *zing*.

Then I thought of Zakopane.

And of *Where Eagles Dare*.

As a WWII history-buff, I was familiar with the Zakopane Conferences. I had been appalled at the depths to which human beings could sink in the name of an ideology and self-aggrandizement.

Where Eagles Dare was the second full-length English novel I'd ever read [my first language is Bengali], the first being *Guns of Navarone*. These two books by Alistair MacLean made me fall in love with adventure fiction, a love that is still going strong. While reading *Where Eagles Dare*—and seeing the movie later—I was astonished by the action-sequences, the infiltration of Schloss Adler, the fight on the cable-car, the final reveal of the traitor at the end. After finishing the book, I promised to myself that I would write something like that one day.

Nearly 30 years later, I am finally keeping my promise.

I have taken three licenses. First is the location. I've made my version of Zakopane a resort on top of a mountain. As far as I know, the place is nothing of the sort. And to the best of my knowledge, there's no monorail line operating out of Zakopane in 1939. Finally, there is a place called Budachów, but it's not where I've placed it.

X X X

KAUSHIK KARFORMA—My fascination with and love for genre fiction was kindled by Alistair MacLean, Desmond Bagley, and Jack Higgins. Robert Ludlum and Eric van Lustbader nurtured that love. But it was a dog-eared book that I picked up on a whim at used-book store in Calcutta (the city in eastern India where I was born, and live and work) that really opened my eyes to the wonderful, wonderful world of high-octane thrillers. That book was called *The List* and belonged to the Nick Carter, Killmaster series. From that moment on, I started devouring those books. From Nick Carrer I progressed to Mack Bolan, then to Able Team and Phoenix Force. Then came Remo Williams—the original, bat-shit crazy, totally un-PC series—followed by Matt Helm, and Sam Durrell. And of course there were the Mark Girland books by James Hadley Chase and the Modesty Blaise books by Peter O'Donnell and the Scarecrow books by

Matthew Reilly. I even managed to read a Death Merchant book. Sadly, till date, it's the only one in the series that I've read.

When ebooks exploded into the scene, I discovered John Rain, John Milton, and a host of excellent self-published books. And all the while, I have been honing my craft, looking for an opportunity to get my writing in front of readers. Thanks to Ron Fortier, I've finally got the opportunity.

Ron, my deepest and most sincere gratitude.

A very big Thank You to Philip Athans, whose online course on the Lester Dent method and insightful blog-posts helped me refine my writing technique.

I would like to dedicate this story to my three-year old daughter Kaushiki, whom I call Gullusaurus (Gullu is her original nickname; I added the 'saurus' because she's like a two-legged Tyranosaurus Rex, always up to some mischief or other.). I hope when she's old enough to read this story, she feels proud of her Dadzilla.

SECRET AGENT "X"

Dead do Dance

by Frank Schildiner

Happy" Jack Jackson was a man who always had a wide smile on his face. Even when he was cutting a throat or firing a Tommy gun at an enemy, the smile never dropped. One of the top killers-for-hire in the city, Happy Jack lived the good life every day of the week.

Today, on this bright spring day, he spread his happiness as he walked through his neighborhood, the legendary slum known as Hell's Kitchen. The scents of dirt, decay, spoiled food, fresh boiled cabbage, cheap liquor filled the air. This was the scent of poverty and despair—a sensation felt by hard-working decent men and women trapped in a life as harsh as the one their families attempted to abandon overseas. Hell's Kitchen as not a forgiving quarter—life was the cheapest commodity and a simmering anger always existed beneath the surface.

Yet Happy Jack Jackson walked through this district, smiling and reveling in his success. The son of a second generation Irish immigrant, he'd been a bad kid from the start. A fighter who earned his cash by thrashing other boys on the street in quick bare-knuckle battles, he took to crime and killing with an ease that amazed even the former boss of the Irish gangs, the legendary Donnie O'Rourke.

With O'Rourke dead, the Irish gangs obeyed the whims of Happy Jack. This was a smart move; he was close to the Five Families and worked as their personal, unofficial killing tool. Money would flow, at least for those close to Happy Jack.

"Good morning, Mister Jackson." People called as he strode past, a large expensive cigar clenched in the corner of his teeth.

"Call me, Jack." He replied, accepting small token gifts like a baron among his serfs. He handed out small bills and coins randomly, patted the cheeks of little girls and boys and spoke with gentle politeness to the elderly. People accepted the tokens, their smiles tight, their eyes betraying their terror of this wolf in sheep's clothing.

"Hey, Smiley. You swallow a feather or something?" A rough, familiar voice called.

Happy Jack started and spun, his hand reaching for the .45 automatic he always wore under his arm. His mouth dropped in shock and he was momentarily unable to move. "You?"

"That's right, yah smiling bastard." The man snarled back, pointing a heavy Tommy gun at Happy Jack. He was a short man with curly black hair, a pencil mustache and the battered face of prize fighter. He wore an expensive silk shirt, a tailored blue pin-striped suit, and a pearl-grey fedora pulled low and slightly to the side. "Remember me? I'm back."

Before Happy Jack could respond, the expensively clad man giggled with mad laughter and fired. The Thompson sub-machine spat, the bullets chewing through the air and ripping into Happy Jack Jackson. The killer laughed as he continued to pour bullets into the fallen corpse of the boss of Hell's Kitchen.

Then suddenly he stopped. Pausing to check his look in the reflection of a store front. Pausing to wave to an elderly man seated on a nearby stoop, the killer strode away, whistling tunelessly and vanished around a corner. Slowly people emerged from their homes, hearing the sirens blare as they stared down at the body of Happy Jack Jackson.

X X X

At the same time Happy Jack died in a hail of bullets, another event was occurring across town. A short distance away in mileage, but a long journey culturally, existed Chinatown. A district that was spreading into nearby Little Italy, these streets were heavily populated and much like another country. Most shop signs were in Chinese letters and many people did not, or refused to admit, they even spoke English.

Still, life flourished in Chinatown. People worked hard and lived a better life than they had overseas in Asia. Food wasn't scarce and the district was semi-autonomous. Violence occurred, but the internecine warfare between the Tongs ended a few years ago. The infamous San Francisco born gang leader, Sai Wing Mock, better known as Mock Duck, lead his Hip Sing gangsters to ultimate victory. Their formerly powerful rivals, the On Leongs, still existed but were a shadow of their former power.

That was why Eng Shi, the number four man in the formerly great On Leong tong, pushed his way down Mott Street, basically ignored by the populace. People knew his identity, recognized he was a dangerous man who killed in the past and controlled three gambling dens for his gang. They also knew that to pay tribute to his power would be to announce an allegiance to the On Leongs. A poor notion considering the vast control the Hip Sing gang possessed over Chinatown.

A diminutive man with graying hair worn close cropped to his skull, Eng Shi was born a member of his Tong. His grandfather was once the personal bodyguard to the original leader of the gang, the late Tom Lee. Eng Shi's father was a bookkeeper, still employed by an On Leong business in his eighties. And Eng Shi's son was already on his way to joining the brotherhood.

The trouble was the gang was weak these days. They needed to find a method of regaining their power, which was why Eng Shi was heading across Chinatown to look into a new antique dealer that was about to open on Canal Street. That was the type of concern that could attract attention from wealthy members of Manhattan society. They had potential political contacts and power. A way to raise the On Leong's position, if only slightly.

Stepping onto Canal Street, Eng Shi glanced left and right. Though battles and attacks on the street were rare now, they did still occur. Gamblers, especially those that lost heavily, occasionally went mad and attempted to get revenge for their change of fortune. Eng Shi carried a large revolver on his belt at all times.

Crossing over, Eng Shi headed down Canal, seeing the shop in question a short distance away. He was about to continue when he was jostled hard from his right. A blow struck him hard in his midsection and he gasped in pain. A jolt of agony shook Eng Shi's body as he was hit again in the stomach, followed by a strike to the heart.

Distantly, Eng Shi's mind registered the attacks were that of a dagger. He'd been a knife swinging killer in his youth, a standard path for entry into any street gang. Ten Hip Sings died by Eng Shi's blade before he was promoted to a position of power. Now he was learning how that felt—from the other side of the blade.

Tumbling to the sidewalk, he looked up at his attacker. His face, already draining of color from blood loss, turned pale with shock. The figure standing above him was tall, slim, with a face handsome to the point of being girlish and pretty. He wore traditional Chinese clothing and clutched a long, blood-stained highbinder blade in one slim, long-fingered hand. The man's hair was waist length and tied in a que reminiscent of the days of the Q'ing Emperors.

"You—no—this is a dream..." Eng Shi whispered as blood pooled beneath his fallen form.

"No dream, Eng Shi. You see me and I send you to the hell of the piercing hooks," the other replied in a quiet, soft voice. He flicked the blood off his blade and walked down the street, disappearing from sight almost immediately.

Eng Shi died seconds later, but his killer was recognized by several older men in the district...

X X X

At the other end of the city, at exactly the same time Eng Shi was gasping his final breath, Tino Terranova sipped a tiny glass of red wine and sighed contentedly. Life was good for his aging bones. The consiglieri of the Maroni family, one of the most powerful organizations in New York, he'd seen it all. The poverty of living in an apartment with no heat, a shared bathroom, and often no food since the old man died. He'd supported his two brothers and three sisters by stealing; starting with food and later by holding up rich-looking men over in mid-town.

It'd been one of those robberies that got him an association with Paulo Anthony, the then-boss of the family. It seemed, purely by luck, Tino roughed up a competitor in the lucrative plasterer's trade, a man named Witherspoon who couldn't be bought. By busting the guy's arm with a pipe, Tino inadvertently allowed Anthony another chance at getting a partnership in the man's business.

As a member of the Anthony family, Tino Terranova flourished. A smart, if uneducated man, he'd learned fast and knew when to take chances, and when to stay quiet. Tino never aspired to be the boss and always had an instinct for whom to support in any battle for leadership. When the infamous Night of Sicilian Vespers battle happened a few years back, a forty-something Tino Terranova was the first to back Salvatore Maroni. That night he even took up a gun and helped execute three who might dispute the new boss's claims. The payoff was the number three spot in the organization and the closest advisory position to the boss.

Now, mere years later, Tino Terranova knew he had it good. He had a nice stream of income he used to keep his family happy and lived like one of the old barons from back in the old country. Tino wore white linen suits like a rich man and people kissed his hand and begged for his help with problems in their sad little lives. All knew there was blood on his hands; even if he rarely participated in executions anymore. Tino Terranova was a man of respect, you walked softly in his presence and hoped you didn't anger him in any way.

"Another, *padrone*?" the waiter asked, rubbing his hands together and bowing slightly in an obsequious manner.

"*Si, grazi.*" Tino replied and smiled as the waiter filled the glass and replaced the plate of biscotti on the table. The man bowed slightly again and backed away, afraid of making a mistake.

"You like a pig. A fat, pale, lazy, pig." A voice spat in harsh Sicilian. "Look at you, sitting around like you ain't got blood on your soul. You go to church now, piggie?"

Tino Terranova reared up, his face twisted with rage. He reached for the small pistol he always kept tucked in the small of his back. Then he spotted the speaker. A man, about Tino's height, dressed in simple, plain dark peasant's clothing. A thick black mustache covered his sneering lips. He held a heavy sawed-off shotgun in his left hand.

"What is this, some kind of joke?" Tino screamed, momentarily stunned into immobility. His face registered consternation and a growing terror.

"No, it's not *porco giuda*." The mustachioed man snarled and fired both barrels of his gun.

Tino Terranova was blown backwards, knocking his table and chair over, his suit immediately transforming from white to crimson. As he died, he got one final look at his killer, who paused long enough to spit once in his dying eyes.

That completed, the killer walked down the street, whistling a jaunty tune.

X X X

The final killing of the day happened at the same time as the other three.

George "Numbers" Shapiro was a gangster of the old school. A close contact of Corrado Prizzi, he ran the sports betting book with efficiency. A childhood friend of the terrifying head of the syndicate, George listened to Don Corrado when the latter pushed him to get his degree in accounting from Empire State University.

Now, George Shapiro was a wealthy man. Owner of three banks and an accounting firm, he was a rising power in the community. His children were already down for top universities and would be upstanding members of the community. They didn't need to know that while their father was studying for finals, he was also helping the Prizzi family rise to the top of the mafia hierarchy.

Which was why his death was the one that garnered the biggest notice in the newspapers. Though known as a close friend of the Prizzi boss, George Shapiro was not a man the police ever confronted. Even the IRS walked softly, he was a bank owner with political contacts in the city and beyond.

Examining the family position in Mammoth Studios, George decided to diversify. The Wallenquist Organization sought a partnership with the Prizzis in Woltz International Pictures, having the disgusting pedophiliac president of the company under their thumb. A partnership with the Prizzis would enable the Wallenquists to deal with the union issues that plagued the studio and raise the profitability. A good deal, though one George knew would need to be approached with care.

Giving the deal a preliminary yes, George looked up as his huge wooden door flew open. Nobody entered his office without permission, even his wife and children needed to call his formidable secretary, Miss Parkhurst, for an appointment. Miss Parkhurst, a Marine-sized force of nature with the personality of a bad tempered bulldog, yielded to no man or woman. This was an unprecedented moment.

The man stepping into the office was a lean, lithely built character with long legs and a feline grace. His face was triangular and all angles. His thin lips were pulled back into a mad grin. Dressed in expensive, silk clothing with a white fedora tilted rakishly forward, this man was the very picture of the dime store hoodlum.

"Hey there, Numbers. Remember your old pal? I told you no bullet can put me down." The man spoke in a light New York accent, sounding as if he was telling a funny anecdote rather than raising a pair of revolvers.

"Jack? You—you're dead!" George Shapiro said, reaching for a revolver in his top desk drawer.

"Maybe I was, buddy. Not anymore," the man identified as Jack replied and fired both guns. He fired fast and recklessly with only two bullets hitting George Shapiro. Sadly, they were enough to kill him in an instant. The other couple of dozen slugs shredded the desk and wall and one security guard.

Seeing his enemy was dead, the man named Jack tipped his hat to Miss Parkhurst, pirouetted once and left the bank. His smile never diminished as he strode away, not bothering to hide his guns or move with any celerity.

The guard, who took only a small wound to the right arm, was a former cop name Sid Irving. He'd retired as a foot patrol officer; a loyal one who knew what lines to cross. His pension wasn't bad, but the bank job made life easier. It also meant he had a place to go every day; the reason he and his old lady still got along.

Sid Irving wasn't worried that the police would be informed, one of the tellers was still on the phone with the local precinct. They could let the mobsters know what happened this day. No, Sid had to let someone else know. Someone very important and Sid Irving's real employer.

The man known as Secret Agent X.

X X X

It wasn't long before the reports trickled in from the four high-profile killings in the city, all at precisely one o'clock in the afternoon. Four gangsters, older men in each case, publicly murdered in plain sight. The killers not only didn't bother to hide, they appeared to almost revel in being seen and identified by those in their respective neighborhood.

The first interview recorded was with Sid Irving as the paramedics patched up his arm. The former officer was seated in an ambulance as a youngish Detective Inspector named Joe repeatedly asked him the same questions, attempting to find a hole in the man's story.

"Stop saying that, it's a load of hooey. How many pain pills did they give you?" Inspector Joe barked after Sid's third assertion of the man named Jack's identity.

"None, yet. I'm not crazy. It was—" Sid asserted.

X X X

Almost at the same time Joe was deciding between demanding Sid Irving either be checked for drinking on the job or be sent to Bellevue in a straightjacket, Finn O'Rourke was gesticulating madly as he spun his tale. All knew Finn was a watcher, spending his days seated on his stoop, keeping an eye on everything in the neighborhood. He wasn't much of a storyteller, preferring to just sit, smoke and stare.

Now, with the body of Happy Jack only ten feet away and the police sirens still blaring as they weaved through the Kitchen, Finn O'Rourke was a changed man. Wild-eyed and talking non-stop, he was the only true witness of the events.

"I said to myself, it's can't be him 'cause he's dead. Then he looked my way and I know it's him. I'm telling you, he's back." Finn babbled, almost incoherent with fright. "It was—"

X X X

In Chinatown, the police were present, but nobody was speaking to the men in blue. The lack of trust in the community for the police was a long-standing issue, with very few officers capable of bridging the gap. The current captain, an unseen figure named Captain Green, was more interested in using his assignment as a stepping stone to a deputy chief's uniform. His method was to order regular rousts of young Chinese men and to occasionally arrest a gangster.

This was why an elderly man named Sung Tse-Ho requested an audience with the two tong gangsters he knew. Both were men close to his age,. One a member of the powerful Hip Sings; the other a former hatchet man for the On Leongs. No secret was made of this meeting, it taking place in the well-known Port Arthur Restaurant.

Both men—the Hip Sing only called Kwan and the On Leong, known as Liu—respected the elderly Sung Tse-Ho, but found this very unusual. All three sat at the same time to save face and the two tong men remained silent. Unhurried, Sung Tse-Ho poured two cups of tea, presenting both to the gangsters at the same time. He then poured his own and toasted both men.

"I called you both here out of respect. I witnessed the killing on Eng Shi. You may consider me an old fool when I tell you the identity of the murderer. Please believe me, I tell you both out of respect to both your brotherhoods. You see, the killer of Eng Shi was—" Sung Tse-Ho stated, bowing his head to both men.

✕ ✕ ✕

Uptown, where Tino Terranova's murder took place, the waiter, a man named Emmanuel Pipi, told his story to two of the hulking monsters employed by Boss Moroni. The two men, only known as Jerry and Tony, towered over the tiny Emmanuel, their quart bottle sized fists raised threateningly before the terrified man's face.

"I'm not pazzo, sirs! I'm not! I saw him, plain as my face!" Emmanuel Pipi pleaded. He knew one punch from these men could kill him easily.

These bruisers didn't realize that the man they were threatening could no more lie in the face of physical violence than he could play shortstop for the Yankees. Emmanuel Pipi was not a well man—at least he believed in that in his heart and soul. The son of a tough, hard-working baker, Emmanuel was the youngest of six in a family that also included his grandmother, a maiden aunt and an uncle who stole for a living. A sickly child, he discovered early that if he was sick, his family coddled him to the exclusion of the others. Later, he married Ana Vitale, who loved mothering him and treating Emmanuel for his many imagined illnesses.

"I don't think he's fooling." Tony said, looking at his partner.

Emmanuel Pipi shook his head quickly, looking at the giant men with pleading, puppy dog eyes. "I'd never lie to you two or to Don Salvatore. The man who did this was—"

✕ ✕ ✕

"Legs Diamond," Sid Irving insisted again to Inspector Joe. He'd said the same to Secret Agent X moments before and received the same response.

X X X

"Yee Toy who we all used to call Girlface." Sung Tse-Ho stated, lowering his head slightly more, knowing he would be seen as an old, insane fool by these men.

X X X

"Mad Dog Vinnie Coll himself, large as life and madder than ever!" Finn O'Rourke cried again to his listeners.

X X X

"Don Giuseppe Morello. We used to call him Clutch Hand because his fingers on his right hand was like a big claw." Emmanuel Pipi whispered, making his hand resemble the one he viewed earlier,

X X X

"He's dead." Was the universal sentiment from the listeners, all of whom looked at the witnesses with open incredulity. There were some variations in each case—with Inspector Joe supplying the details that the infamous Jack "Legs" Diamond was gunned down years ago in Albany, New York.

The listeners in Chinatown rolled their eyes at the elderly man's tale, leaving without bothering to answer his claims. All in Chinatown knew of the death many years ago of the killer called Yee Toy. A beautiful, almost effeminate looking man, he'd been responsible for at least forty deaths in the Hip Sing/On Leong wars. His death in 1919 was hailed as good for the whole world, not to mention Chinatown.

Finn O'Rourke's tale faced open mockery from the residents of Hell's Kitchen. The dead did not return to life, that was the universal belief. To suggest otherwise was to either invoke scary films or even, in some case, blasphemy. Yet the elderly man held to his story until the day he died, falling off the stoop on VE Day.

As to the suspicious gangsters of the Morelli family, they rolled their

"He's dead" was the universal sentiment...

eyes and reported their tale to the boss. The wildly held belief was a faker pretended to be the murdered old gangster who once ran the family. A search was made of the Italian and Sicilian enclaves of the Five Boroughs of the City without results.

Yet one man believed—sensing a bigger issue at hand. The hidden protector of the United States, Secret Agent X.

X X X

Seated in his sanctuary beneath the city, Secret Agent X sat before a mirror and assembled his new identity. The Agent was known, to the few who even realized his existence, as the Man of a Thousand Faces. This title was not undeserved. Only one other man in the world possessed the sheer genius of makeup and impersonation as Secret Agent X. That other, another hero, had his own agenda and they did not interact or even acknowledge each other's operation.

The handful of people who learned the true face of X would not recognize him now. He examined himself one further time and stood, changing into a suit from his racks of clothing exclusively for disguise. Today, instead of a tall, powerfully athletic man, the Agent was transformed completely.

Stepping into the exit that lead to a busy subway platform was a shorter, rounder man with ruddy cheeks, salt and pepper hair, old food stains on his tie and a growing paunch. His nose was the shape and color of a boiled potato and the Agent walked with a rolling lumber.

Secret Agent X was now in the guise of Sgt. Oscar Taylor, an experienced homicide officer who, in fact, never existed. This was an identity X created over the years, appearing at times to write a report and help solve a simple murder. This backup identity was necessary; all of his living police identities were called into headquarters after the rash of murders. Time to activate Taylor and learn the full extent of the wave of killings.

One of X's favorite identities was in place, bustling around and haranguing anyone sitting still. Commissioner Foster, a blocky blond haired man, appeared annoyed by the information he kept receiving.

"Four crooks killed on the street. And all you geniuses got for me is three names of men dead and buried for years! How about that one dead in Chinatown?" Foster asked, his voice a rising tone of rage.

"Nobody saw nothing, nobody heard nothing." A man dressed in Captain's bars replied, shrugging. "Chinatown don't talk."

Foster leaned in on the man. "You going to settle for that? Start busting down every door and speaking to every crook in the state! You got me?" Foster practically screamed.

X picked that time to gather a copy of the files and exit the main detective floor of Police Plaza. The copies were poor, typed and retyped carbon copies of the four reports and witness statements. This was not a test to Agent X; he was used to such conditions in emergencies. His training in the Great War covered this usually unconsidered issue in the life of an intelligence agent.

In the time it took most men or women to read and comprehend one of the folders, X's keen mind memorized all four. The victims were all men known to him, were part of his extensive files on the criminals who inhabited New York. In those criminal archives X recorded known fact as well as rumors, suppositions, and considerations. This method of detailing was one of his many lessons in his quest to become a warrior against the black evils of crime and espionage. His teacher in this area was a master detective without peer—a formidable, if quirky, English-born genius.

Staring at the ceiling, X recalled all the information in his own files regarding these men, the rumors of their activities towards others as well as their deaths. Thousands of lines of facts and suppositions crossed his mind at an uncanny rate. Agent X's agile mind pieced together the disparate data in mere moments. The answer arrived and he realized he'd spent almost an hour staring upward—the only signs of life in his body a slow steady breathing and a pursing of his lips.

The answer was before his eyes, a message from the conscious and unconscious mind. All but one point; a final confirmation not apparent in his data. For that he needed to beard one of the most dangerous men in the United States. The horrible, terrifying, and uncannily dangerous master of the Hip Sing tong—the man known to the world as Mock Duck.

Stepping out of the unused office, Agent X nearly bumped into the rampaging Commissioner Foster. Looking him up and down, the political boss of Manhattan law enforcement snarled.

"You taking a nap in there? Get your rear on the street or I'll have you walking a beat by the docks in the middle of a blizzard!"

Agent X nodded and said, "Yes, sir Mister Commissioner." And left the complex. He had a new look to assemble before heading into Chinatown.

X X X

Park Avenue apartments were the most sought after real estate in the city. They represented the extremes of wealth and position. They were not nearly as large as the majestic old homes of the robber baron families of the nineteenth century. Nor were they as well-appointed as the brownstones in the same neighborhood. Despite these limitations, to say you resided in a Park Avenue dwelling was considered by most of the city to be the highest place in Manhattan society.

At least that was the theory. To Benny Molnar his place represented the ultimate failures of his family. He stared with open revulsion at the two-floor penthouse on 55 Central Park West and knew he, and his whole family were nothing but failures. The penthouse, though spacious and filled with expensive furnishings, was less impressive than those of the nearby Dakota building. The antiques were showy, glitzy, and frankly quite vulgar. Which was a perfect demonstration of the Molnar clan and their lesser place in the world.

Benny Molnar was the son of Anton Molnar, a Hungarian immigrant who arrived in the United States with a pair of shoes and asset of clothing two sizes too big. He'd been recruited by a gang mere days after arriving, rising to the position of boss in mere months. A friend of many of the top gang leaders, he formed a shipping business that eventually became a prime supplier of bootleg booze from Canada and Scotland. When Prohibition ended Anton Molnar went legitimate, banking his many millions and merging his business with an older, more established firm. The former gangster took up golf, hotel ownership and living the easy life.

Anton's only goal after that was to ensure a good life for his family. His first son, Herman, was smart enough to gain a spot in Columbia medical school. He was now a heart surgeon in Miami and was the pride of the family. His daughter, Miriam, was a writer and college professor in New Jersey. More importantly, to Anton, she'd given birth to three wonderful grandchildren. But her academic achievements were nice too.

Only Benny, real name Benjamin Kiss Molnar, was a disappointment. Benny, an angry child who disliked work, studying or listening to anyone's rules, was a failure in every area. He spent his days sleeping and going out to night clubs and other mob run business after. The gangsters found him amusing and a little pathetic—recognizing that Benny wanted to be one of their members but was incapable of doing any of the duties needed to help a crime family. Only the very low-end family, the savage, unintelligent, Bocchicchio clan allowed him to serve among their ranks. Even they didn't find Benny capable of anything other than as a driver and a body to stand in a group during negotiations with the bigger families.

This only served to fuel Benny's rage. He wanted—nay he burned—to be more than a low-level nothing in a family considered a joke by the other crime clans. Benny Molnar dreamed of being the boss of bosses, the master of all crime throughout the nation. To be the man who all crime families obeyed was closest a man could get to be a Roman emperor or a feudal king. He was the lord of life and death, any whim that struck his fancy was granted; women, luxurious living, the respect of the masses.

At least this was Benny Molnar's theory and belief. His father never discussed his former profession, only stating that, "the past was the past." His former associates were also closed mouth men, viewing talkers and tale-tellers as people ill-suited for their profession.

Which meant Benny's beliefs emerged entirely from his imagination. Movies from Hollywood, books—and most importantly, thriller magazines—showed how these master criminals were the modern equivalents of royalty. That they were destroyed by the heroes and cops in those stories was, in Benny's opinion, just wishful thinking on the part of the publishers. True bosses were untouchable and the legendary boss of bosses was a being of great majesty. Simply put, Benny Molnar was a delusional, spoiled, rich kid with little to no understanding of the world of organized crime.

This might have remained a fantasy for the rest of Benny's life had he not agreed to take a boat trip to the islands. There, on his parent's boat off the coast of Haiti, he met the man who promised to help him realize his dreams. If he could ever get the man to listen to his suggestions. His first follower, one who would transform the world in Benny's favor.

Seeing his follower seated at the big wooden desk, one of his father's favorite furnishings, Benny Molnar snarled. "What are you doing? I ordered you to get to work!"

"I did, my friend. I did. Go and check the newspapers. You will see much that will surprise you this day." The latter smiled and returned to reading from a massive elderly leather-bound book stolen from a New England college.

Benny was momentarily stunned, not used to be brushed aside so easily. Without a word, he turned on his heels and left. The headlines from the New York Globe, New York Herald, and the New York Gazette pulled him in and did represent a first step towards his plan. Master of the mob!

X X X

Heading into Chinatown was never an easy task for Secret Agent X. Though this was a part of the city, open for free travel like any other part of New York, there was a sensation at times of entering another country. The Asian enclave was like the infamous Kowloon Walled City slum of Hong Kong, though far more sanitary. The people of Chinatown resided in astonishingly close quarters and maintained their cultural identity despite their disconnection from their homeland. Most visitors to Chinatown were amazed by the transformation of the streets and style, marveled at the quaint differences between this neighborhood and the rest on Manhattan. They also stayed on the busy public avenues such as Canal, Pell and Mott streets, aware of their outsider status.

For Secret Agent X the differences were even more profound. When he traveled to Chinatown, he did so for either information or to hunt down an evil-doer. The latter allowed him to behave as he chose, disguise as he preferred and ignore the customs and mores of the area. In the hunt for villains, Agent X would take any steps required to defeat his enemy. Years earlier, he'd operated undercover as a curio dealer named Ling, his makeup skills enabling him to get close to the representative of the Lord of Strange Deaths and defeat their plans for New York.

Seeking information was a far more difficult matter. To disguise himself as one of the residents, or even a visitor from abroad could be taken as an insult by the dangerous men he sought to entreat. At the same time, X was well-aware he could not place himself in the power of any of the warlords who ruled this district of Manhattan.

As such, X changed into a simple disguise, that of a tall man with dark hair, a tailored grey suit and bronze skin. His eyes were now hazel colored and he kept an obvious .45 automatic under his arm. He was now very dangerous looking, possibly a mercenary or a representative of a criminal group.

Heading into Chinatown, he walked directly for a small, multi-story building that looked like any other in the city. Next to a series of simple brick faced storefronts was a doorway—one easy to miss in the hustle, bustle of the always busy Pell Street. Situated next to the door was a simple brass plate with the Chinese characters spelling out "Hip Sing Association."

This innocuous looking dwelling was the headquarters of one of the most dangerous crime organizations in the United States. The Hip Sings, under the control of the terrifying Sai Wing Mock alias Mock Duck, were the masters of every Chinatown in the country. No crime was too great for this tiny fraction of the American Chinese populace. Even the other crime groups in the city and other locations left these fierce criminals alone.

Agent X knew one day he would need to battle these bloodstained crooks. But not today. For now he needed information and nobody was better able to fulfill this need. The danger was great, but the need was greater.

Knocking on the door, X was unsurprised to be greeted by two men, each openly carrying revolvers. The two were a head shorter than X, dressed in inexpensive suits and had their short hair cut close to their heads. They were both thin to the point of emaciation, but the fierce glint in their eyes denoted a fanatical willingness to do without food in favor of their duty. They didn't speak, instead they merely stared in his direction, and waited.

"Sai Wing Mock, if you please." X stated in clear Cantonese.

The man on the right shook his head. "Nobody here by that name. Go away, gwailo."

Agent X chuckled at the insult. Gwailo meant "ghost face" and was meant to be very derogatory. He could spit back a series of insults worthy of a Hong Kong stevedore, but he didn't have time. Instead he rolled his eyes and stated, "Does it look like I care what you say? Take me to Mock Duck. I come bearing gifts."

"Wait here." The man on the right said and closed the door. They were gone for five minutes, when the door opened again. This time an older man, about forty years old, dressed in finer, cleaner clothing was in front. The two guards were a step behind, their guns raised but un-cocked.

"Your gun?" He asked in unaccented English. "No man enters this building armed."

X opened his jacket and allowed one of the guards to take his weapon. He wasn't worried; the weapon was specifically to be taken. The other guard patted him down, extracting a small wrapped box about the size of a man's finger. He handed the item to the older man and bowed, returning to his position.

"What business do you have with the Hip Sing Association?" The older man asked.

X shook his head. "My words are only for the leader of your brotherhood."

The older man looked annoyed for a moment, but then composed himself to an expression of neutrality. "Very well. Follow me."

Agent X fell into step behind one bodyguard, another at his rear. They strode through a series of corridors before coming to a halt in a small office. The older man took a seat behind the desk and nodded.

The bodyguard at X's rear raised his gun and placed the barrel against the Agent's skull, snickering softly. The other bodyguard turned and pointed his gun at Agent X's chest and smiled a grin full of malice.

The older man crossed his arms across his chest. "Kill him now. We will leave him as an example to others. No man makes demands of the Hip Sing Tong."

Both bodyguards cocked the triggers of their revolvers, their fingers tightened on the triggers. At this distance, neither could miss…

X X X

The Jacobi floating poker game was a Brooklyn tradition. A game that started in 1919 on the same day legendary gambler Arnold Rothstein fixed the World's Series, the game appeared every week since that time. A high stakes game supported by two of the crime families, it was an institution of the city.

Tonight's game took place in a small detached home in Red Hook. The house was for sale, the owner choosing to move in with her son in New Jersey. The lawyer in charge of the sale owed Leon Jacobi—the current proprietor of the game, son of Meyer Jacobi the founder—and volunteered the house as payment for the small debt. Leon moved his people in, transforming the empty shell into a comfortable, classy, understated poker hall. Three dealers stood ready on staff, replaced randomly every thirty to forty-five minutes. A bartender, two waitresses and a pair of armed guards stood ready to prevent trouble. The local police received a generous donation from Leon and five of the biggest players in a three-state radius received special chauffer driven cars to the location.

All was good, two hours into the game nobody was bust yet, nor was anyone a clear winner. A player named Chicago Gus was ahead, but only by three hundred dollars. Leon sat back, watching and calculating his percentages based on the amount of money on the table. If all went as it should, he should pocket thirty thousand dollars after all payoffs. Easy way to make a living, all he had to do was keep the game honest. The house, he and his backers, always made a profit that way.

He was just beginning to calculate the exact amount, when the door opened and the loud chatter of Tommy-gun fire filled the air. The bodyguard on the door fell, his body riddled with bullets. Mad Dog Coll stepped inside, laughing and firing his gun at all present. The gamblers dropped to the ground, trying to hide from the onslaught.

Leon dove to the ground near the gamblers, reaching for the small gun he always wore in his belt. As he pulled it free, he watched the bartender and all three dealers drop to the ground, their eyes wide, their bodies stained crimson with their lifeblood.

Legs Diamond was a few steps behind Mad Dog, a pair of .45 automatics in hand.

He shot down the waitresses and then systematically executed each gambler with one shot to the head. He holstered one of his guns and scooped up the bank under one arm. Looking down at the cowering Jacobi, Legs smiled and nodded, "You must be little Leon. You remember me? I knew your dad. I'll let you go this time. Tell your buddies that Vince Coll and Jack Diamond are back. They better retire or they're dead too. Got me?"

Leon Jacobi nodded, stunned and unable to speak. He remembered Jack Legs Diamond. His dad was afraid of the man, a renowned killer and bootlegger who possessed an uncanny ability to survive any battle. This was the man, even down to the mocking intonations of his voice.

"Good lad. Maybe you can work for us when we take over." Legs favored him with another smile, pirouetted in a quick graceful circle, and headed out. Mad Dog Coll stared down at Leon with dead eyes, his hands tight on his machine gun. A moment later, he turned away and was gone.

Leon Jacobi crawled to the telephone, not sure how he could explain the presence of two of gangland's most infamous killers. Both of whom were known to be long dead…

X X X

The click of the revolvers filled the air and X exploded into action. Dropping into a full split, the bullet from the revolver at his rear nearly creased his skull but missed by mere inches. The slug struck the wall behind the seated man just as the second gun roared. The bullet from this gun hammered into the chest of the gangster at Agent X's rear, causing the man to cry out and tumble backwards. His gun fell to the floor, snatched up by X. He fired once at the shocked gangster, hitting the Tang warrior's revolver and sending the weapon sailing across the room.

X rose and unloaded the weapon. Pocketing the bullets, he tossed the revolver aside. He crossed his arms across his chest. "Now that we completed that, please bring me to Mock Duck."

He shot down the waitress...

The older gangster looked momentarily annoyed, his faced flushed and his fist gripped the edge of his desk with white-knuckled intensity. He looked as if he was about to spit out an oath in response or reach for a hidden weapon. Then he composed himself, snatched up the small gift X carried in and stood. A moment later he led Agent X up a set of stairs and past several heavily armed guards, who watched him with open curiosity. They stopped before a large metal door with no visible knob or lock.

The older man knocked three times, paused and tapped an odd tattoo on the metal frame. There was another short pause and he performed the ritual again. After three times, the door slowly opened with a creak and a pair of men carrying Tommy guns stepped into view. They were each dressed in white suits with red ties and pearl fedora pulled low over their foreheads. They appeared to be the very image of Hollywood gangsters, though with Asian features.

"Is this mug carrying a rod?" The man on the left asked, his voice a clear impression of the legendary gangster, Rico Bandello.

The older man shook his head and answered in Cantonese. "No, we took that away. He is well-trained in fighting."

"That hand stuff can't stop me and my Chicago typewriter." The gangster said and waved them inside with his heavy, black metal gun. He looked up at Agent X and continued. "Don't try no funny stuff, mug. You got me?"

X nodded stepped into the room. This was a large chamber, a rectangular wooden box with a table down the center. Seated at the far end of the room was the legendary "Mayor of Chinatown", the kingpin of the Hip Sings, Sai Wing Mock. The infamous and terrifying Mock Duck.

Mock Duck was a short man with an oval face, a long bulbous nose and unlined skin despite his advanced age. His squinting eyes examined Agent X minutely and his wide mouth was twisted in a smirk that was both amused and sinister. He carried himself with the calm self-assurance of an ancient noble, a man who rose to the purple through the death of his enemies in battle.

"I know you, nameless one. You possess another face and build of a stranger. Yet I know better. Last year you incommoded me; a month after that I was inconvenienced by you; at the end of that year I was hampered in my plans. Now you come to my home and seek me out publicly? I should have you tortured and place your skull as a trophy on my desk." Mock Duck stated, his words spoken in a flat, unemotional tone.

"Paraphrasing Conan Doyle? I am surprised. In any event, I came openly and even brought a visiting gift. I come to you merely for information that will benefit you in the end. Girlface Yee Toy murdered Eng Shi."

Agent X stated, ignoring the others in the room.

"Yee Toy died in 1919. Eng Shi was believed to be his killer. I buried him myself—he was my oldest friend." Mock Duck spat back, his face twisted with rage.

Agent X briefly explained the events of the afternoon and his theory. "Did your witness truly identify the killer as Yee Toy. Or was this just a rumor?"

Mock Duck frowned and did not answer for a moment. Finally, he said, "Yes. Identified by a man who knew my old friend."

"Then somehow he and the other gangsters are back. Thank you, I will confront this problem." Agent X bowed slightly, his eyes never leaving Mock Duck's face.

Mock Duck waved one pudgy hand. "Please do. That creature is not my old friend, but a creature using his body. Leave now."

Agent X did not reply, but moments later was back on Pell Street. He wasn't surprised to see a young Chinese man in a muted blue suit following him at a discreet distance.

X X X

Benny Molnar frowned at the money Legs Diamond placed on his desk. The man stood before him, his eyes cloudy and vacant, his movements slow and clumsy. Legs didn't breathe or even blink. He just stared at a spot on the wall above Benny's head.

"Get out of here. Go back to the room with the others." Benny's face didn't hide his revulsion for this walking corpse.

Legs Diamond didn't respond or even move. He was completely different from the bright flashy figure that left the penthouse hours earlier. He and Mad Dog Coll were laughing and making bad jokes about leaving a trail of corpses to mark their way back home.

Now he just stood and stared, a well-dressed fleshy statue. No human reactions or even biological functions were apparent.

"Hey! You! Get out of my office! I'm the boss here and you listen to me!" Benny stepped up and slapped Diamond's face with a weak backhanded blow. The dead gangster did not move or respond. He merely continued to stare at the wall.

"He does not obey your will, my friend. Only I have the power to command the dead." The other man stated, not rising from his seat on a sofa near the door.

"I'm the boss here! Remember that! I rescued you from the ocean and even got you the crap you needed to bring these killers back. I'm the boss, not you!" Benny Molnar screamed, spittle flying from his mouth as he ranted.

"Of course, my friend." The man said and negligently waved a hand to dismiss Legs Diamond. The shambling undead man slowly trudged from the room—heading back to the distant maid's closet where he and his fellows were stored.

"Good! Don't you forget it! Now why did you send them out to kill some nobody in the middle of nowhere? First you made them go kill some old nobodies. Now they're killing and taking money that I don't need. I told you I wanted them to kill Boss Maroni, Don Prizzi, Roth, and—"

The other man cut him off with a rise of one of his Luciferian eyebrows. "I wished to test the distance I could send my—forgive me—*your* men. These are no mere zombies. They possess much of who they were before death. I believe this is a most miraculous demonstration of my power. But, I am satisfied. Who do you wish dead first?"

Benny Molnar frowned and rubbed his jaw in thought. There were so many men and women he wished to kill, to make payment for their mockery of his dreams and ambition. There was one, he thought, a sneering son of wealth, who secretly controlled a confederation of gangs from his expensive estate. "Big Man. I asked him for a job and he laughed in my face. Told me he wouldn't give me a job mowing his grass."

The other man nodded and rose. Slowly he raised his arms to waist level and cupped his hands together—right hand on top of the left, fingers knotting together. His left thumb slowly rose and lay atop his right-hand knuckles, the gesture very ritualistic and filled with significance.

A moment later, his hand dropped and his thin lips twisted into a rictus smile. "It is done, my friend. My undead assassins shall leave shortly and do as you ask."

"They're *my* men, remember?" Benny Molnar replied, grinning at the thought of the Big Man's death.

"Of course, my friend. Of course they are," Murder Legendre replied and lightly chuckled as he watched Benny Molnar strut about the room.

X X X

The police radio was full of inconsequential reports as Agent X sat reading. The book on magical practices by Oliver Haddo was a turgid read. He did list a few possible means of bringing the dead back, most of which were merely rumors. X snorted and tossed the book aside, reaching for another from his occult collection. He disliked the concept of magic, but knew many evil men and women were prone to using such powers to control humanity. Best to be acquainted with such practices since this appeared to be the case.

At the same time, he was listening to many voices. Agent X's secret web was spreading throughout the New York/New Jersey area. His skills with electronics allowed him to listen in on any radio frequency in this zone. He also had secret wires on certain telephone exchanges, only activated when required. More important than this were the women and men who voluntarily provided him with information, realizing their unseen patron was a warrior fighting against the terrible monsters who wished to enslave mankind. These loyal secret soldiers did not even know the alias Secret Agent X, but served with the knowledge that their shadowy leader only sought to save lives.

A vacuum tube rattled, disgorging a shiny, six-inch, metal capsule. There appeared to be no opening in the bright steel, as if the metallic lozenge was cast as one piece. Agent X ran sensitive fingers down the sides, finding the slight indentations in the metal. He pressed in an exact sequence, knowing that to perform this action incorrectly would trigger a tiny incendiary explosive that would destroy anything within the cylinder.

The capsule swung open and a simple note was within, written in a shaky hand: "I saw Legs Diamond and the Mad Dog walking up Park." The note was unsigned, but X knew the writer was a doorman of an expensive apartment complex. He'd lost a sister as a child because of a gun battle between gangs in his neighborhood and had despised criminals ever since. Nearly blind without his glasses he was unable to serve as a police officer. A loyal man, he was dedicated to the destruction of crime and the men who chose that as a life.

Minutes later, a second metal capsule appeared. This one was from a peanut vendor in Central Park, a jolly fat man name Patrice. He never explained why he despised crime and criminals, but to mention the name of any gangster would result in the man spitting in disgust.

This was all Agent X needed, there was only one place these possibly undead criminals were headed, the Upper East side mansion of the gangster secretly known as the Big Man.

Leaping to his feet, X ran for an exit he rarely used. This was the only way he might beat these killers to their date with murder!

X X X

Two armed guards stood at the gates of the Big Man's mansion, a pair of massive men in dark suits with heavy overcoats and black homburg hats. They stared at every pedestrian with suspicious eyes, their heads swiveling every direction in quick sharp movements. Neither attempted to conceal the heavy shotguns they held under their arms. Behind them was a fifteen-foot-high gate, a relic from the days when the streets were filled with carriages and wagons rather than automobiles. A heavy chain held the gates closed and a large black car blocked the entryway. Across the small, perfectly coiffed lawn wandered men, dressed exactly as the pair on the gate. These men didn't bother to hide their shotguns and Tommy guns.

In the third-floor study, the man known in the organized crime world as the Big Man, poured himself another brandy. These recent moves by a bunch of men pretending to be dead criminals had him on edge. Someone was challenging his spot as the top man in the city. That hadn't happened since Rico Bandello, and he was determined to end it fast.

"You think it's that fake banker, Lonnegan?" O'Bannon asked, straightening his jacket. A heavyset man whose actual job was that of a political boss, he was one of the few advisors the Big Man spoke to directly.

The Big Man thought for a moment and shook his head. "No. This is too—complicated. If Lonnegan made a coup attempt, he'd do so with one of his assassins. The man collects odd killers who attack by surprise. No, this plan is involved and outlandish."

"It's working," O'Bannon replied. "You doubled your guards and all the gangs are on edge. War could happen at any time."

The Big Man nodded slowly. He was a tall man with a fleshy face that was beginning to develop jowls. He possessed patrician features and an accent that sounded more at home in a yacht club than ordering the death of rival gangsters. The son of a failing Mayflower family, he'd discovered a talent for crime and organizing criminals in his teens. It hadn't taken long for him to take control of a small gang and lead them to the top of the gangland structure. Now the Big Man—the only name he allowed his associates to call him—was a wealthy, powerful man who was viewed as one of the country's most important people.

"Maybe so," The Big Man replied, considering ways to make this useful to him.

That was when the gunshots began…

X X X

"Hey! Frenchie!" Benny yelled, running down the hall and pushing into the study. Nobody was in the room, which was odd since Murder Legendre spent most of his time in that room. Benny moved through every room on the floor without finding the sorcerer. Reaching for the phone, he called downstairs, learning that the odd-looking man hadn't left the building.

Confused, Benny walked upstairs and looked out the glass doors. He hadn't expected to see Legendre on the open-air patio, yet there the man sat. In Benny's own chair, staring out into space.

Opening the door, Benny stormed out. "Who told you that you could come up here? This is my floor!"

Murder Legendre smiled slightly, his split mustache and goatee beard twitching before growing still. He did not even look Benny Molnar's direction, but continued to stare forward, his elongated fingers slowly weaving odd patterns in the air.

Benny was astonished, his face growing red in his fury. He'd known Legendre for a year now. The odd-looking sorcerer claimed to be grateful and promised to use his powers to help grant Benny's every wish. He'd succeeded so far, having convinced the whole family to stay away from New York and not inquire about Benny's actions. Lately, he'd been showing a tendency towards sarcasm and amusement as to his patron's behavior.

Drawing his gun, Benny fired the huge automatic once in the air. Murder Legendre did not flinch or even look up—his dark eyes never even shifting directions. Benny fired once at the Haitian's feet, the bullet ricocheted off the stone floor and vanished into the night.

Yet Murder Legendre appeared complete unmoved. He did not even glance in Benny's direction. He merely sat in his chair, staring out into space and smiling. His fluttering fingers finally settled and he held them tented together in his lap.

"If you don't answer me now, I'm going to fill your head full of lead!" Benny screamed, his face taking on the look of a spoiled child being denied a slice of cake.

"Please do," Murder Legendre replied, chuckling softly. "Raise your firearm. Do away with me here and now. Take me from this veil of tears that is life."

"I'm going to count to three. If you're not standing up and apologizing to me, I'm going to turn you into a bloody corpse." Benny stated, trying to sound like Tony Camonte from the film *Scarface*.

"Count away, my friend. *Count!*" Legendre replied, turning his head and focusing on Benny for the first time. A trick of the light made it appear as if his dark eyes were glowing. They looked red, like smoldering embers of a fire and the very unnatural quality of these orbs caused Benny to step back a little.

Raising his gun at the seated form, Benny said in a shaking voice, "One, two..."

"*Three*," Murder Legendre added and smiled broadly. His face possessed a demoniac intensity, a terrifying alien nature that was the embodiment of pure, unadulterated evil.

Benny, frightened by this being before him more than ever, stepped back and pulled the trigger. Or at least that was what he meant to do. Instead he merely staggered backwards a step, the gun still extended. His finger would not obey his command and he struggled in vain to fire the gun. "What the—?"

Murder Legendre rose slowly and turned to fully face him, his motions demonstrating infinite patience and complete and utter amusement. He stared at Benny as he agonized over his finger's unwillingness to move.

Benny, with a howl of annoyance, switched the gun over to his other hand and tried again. With the same lack of results, his finger simply unmoving and not obeying his mental command. Benny switched fingers, trying even with his pinky to no avail.

"Drop the gun." Murder Legendre intoned, his face no longer smiling. Yet the uncanny luminescence of his gaze was still present, filling the staring Benny Molnar with a wave of cold dread.

Benny's hands obeyed the Haitian magician's command, despite his desire to do otherwise. The weapon fell to the floor. "What is going on? What did you do?"

Legendre slowly shrugged his shoulders. "I removed your will. It is what a master does to his disobedient servants."

"Servant? Servant? Look here pal, you work for me! I saved your life; I gave you a bed, a roof over your head and anything you needed to get your magic crap back. This is how you repay me? I'm the boss here, me! You do what I tell you or you die!" Benny ranted, stooping and reaching for his gun.

"Stand up...slave." Murder Legendre ordered, his voice suddenly hard.

Benny Molnar straightened, standing at attention like a soldier. His eyes went wide and he opened his mouth to begin screaming.

"Silence," Legendre said, his odd accent drawing out the sound. "I have heard enough of your talk. Slaves do not talk, they serve. And you,

Benjamin Kiss Molnar, are my slave."

Benny struggled, trying to speak. His mouth and throat would not obey his orders, causing him to release a low, sniveling moan that was almost inaudible. His eyes were wild with fear and his face twisted in something approaching rage.

"You struggle? How very interesting. There is more of you alive than I thought possible. You, my friend, were my first. First of a new breed of zombie. You were my experiment, one that succeeded more than my wildest dreams. I and I alone discovered the secret of a class of the undead who retain their personalities. You see, my friend, you were transformed the night I discovered the formulae in the Book of Eibon we stole." Murder Legendre purred, smiling again at the expression on Benny's face.

"You wish to speak? Be my guest, speak!" Murder Legendre added, fluttering his fingers in a small arc.

Benny gasped and exploded, "You're lying! You drugged me! I can't be dead! I'm Benny Molnar, the boss of bosses—"

He was cut off by another gesture by Legendre. "You are alive, are you? When was the last time you ate a meal? Or woke in your soft bed? Can you remember? You cannot! That is because, the dead do not eat or sleep, my friend. I merely push you into a closet and ignore you until you are needed. I sleep in your bed. I eat your food. You, my foolish friend, are dead."

It was then, after a gesture from the terrifying magus, Benny remembered. Everything rushed back, all the memories since Murder Legendre took over his life. And then he began to shriek with revulsion as to what this terrible, demonic man had done to him since that night...

Murder Legendre watched Benny as he attempted to scream in terror. Then he began to laugh—a wicked sound filled with indescribable evil.

X X X

Spotting the guards at the gate, Mad Dog Coll giggled and opened up with his Tommy gun. He mowed both men down before they could even touch their shotguns and shot down two more standing near the car.

"That's four for the Mad Dog!" he howled, giggling again. "I love turkey shoots!"

Legs Diamond raised his dual automatics and gunned down two approaching gangsters with shotguns. "It ain't a race, pal. Just remember, nobody lives. Especially the high-faluting bastard who runs this joint."

With that, Legs stepped on one of the bodies of the fallen gangsters and pulled himself up and over the gate. He landed on the car's hood and popped off two more shots, killing one man and wounding another. Mad Dog Coll joined him a moment later, squinting at the three story mansion.

"The head of a mob is living in this joint? How's he afford it? When me and my brother was in the business, we never had the cash for a place like this one." Mad Dog said, frowning.

"I hear he's a rich kid that went bad." Legs replied, hopping off the car and stepping over to the man he wounded. The gangster was a heavyset man with a round and a nearly bald head. His hat was in his hand, pressed against the wound in his side—his hand and the fabric were stained crimson with the steadily leaking blood.

"Please," The gangster moaned as Legs approached. "I got a wife and family."

"That's too bad—for them." Legs replied, pirouetted and shot the fallen man once in the forehead.

Mad Dog laughed and fired a burst at a nearby window, shattering the glass. "I like that! Too bad for them. That's funny!"

Legs grinned and bowed. "If I didn't like using my rods and making big money, I'd have been an entertainer. I was a better dancer than any of them acts out there and could make funnier jokes than all four of them Marx Brothers."

"I'd have paid to see that." Mad Dog replied and gunned down two more charging gangsters. He laughed again as they fell, blood splattering across the ground. Mad Dog always laughed when he killed, happiest when he watched the life of an enemy vanish from their bodies. There was something intoxicating about that moment, when he knew that someone was no longer able to live because of his actions. Alcohol, drugs, sex, flashy cars and clothes were all pale shadows of pleasure compared to this sensation. He, Vincent "Mad Dog" Coll was the most powerful being on Earth at that moment. He was the lord of life and death and everyone in his way were merely insects to be trampled underfoot.

"If this is all the Big Man has, his death is going to be as easy as a Sunday stroll." Legs Diamond said, then, a loud crack filled the air and he fell over, a hole between his eyes.

A man stood in the open window, the one Mad Dog had shattered. An M1917 Enfield rifle was held against his shoulder and he shot down Mad Dog three seconds later. His name was Mocco and he was the Big Man's soldier. Not a bright man, he'd spent years training to be an expert with a rifle. This made him permanently useful to the boss; a sniper able to kill from long-distance in one shot.

"Good riddance to bad rubbish," Mocco stated, lowering his rifle with a smile.

"Who you calling trash?" Legs Diamond asked, rising and picking up his fallen guns.

"I think he meant us!" Mad Dog Coll snarled and grabbed his pearl colored fedora. Standing, he snatched up his Tommy gun.

"What the—" Mocco stammered and raised his rifle again. He knew he hit both men bullseye; right in the center of their foreheads. Mocco knew the bullets were perfect, he made them personally and checked each shell. He also knew he'd seen both shots hit home; witnessed the holes in their foreheads—neither of which appeared to bleed…

Before Mocco could fire again, Legs and Mad Dog raised their guns and fired. Their guns blazed as they tore the gangster sniper to pieces, both men continuing to pump lead into the fallen body long after he was dead. What remained could barely be identified as human anymore—the police would later be forced to rely on the blood-spattered and bullet hole ridden identification Mocco carried in his back pocket.

"I don't like sneaks," Mad Dog declared, dropping the heavy, and now empty, ammo drum on the floor.

"Yeah. I killed a few of them when I was fighting the Dutchman." Legs agreed and dropped both of his magazines next to Mad Dog's empty drum.

That was when Secret Agent X jumped out from behind the car and dropped Mad Dog with a kick behind the knee. Before Legs Diamond turned, he struck the gangster with the knife edge of his hand to the back of the neck. A paralyzing blow, one that literally shocked the nervous system.

Yet instead of dropping, Legs Diamond staggered forward and then rubbed the back of his neck with his empty gun.

Mad Dog popped to his feet and swung his heavy, unloaded Tommy gun at X. The Agent stepped aside the attack and fired a punch with his knuckles extended. The blow hit the insane gangster in the throat, destroying the neck bones with an audible snapping sound. Mag Dog dropped his gun as the pain hit him, grabbing his neck with both hands.

"Huh," Legs Diamond mused. "That should have dropped me. I seen Jack Dempsey do the same thing to a creep bothering him one night. Yet it doesn't even hurt much."

"Same here," Mad Dog added, his voice raspier now. "I should be dying like a chicken with his neck wrung. It don't even hurt much."

Agent X didn't wait around to listen to any more talk from the pair of undead killers. He needed to confirm they were no longer alive, not truly

Mad Dog dropped the heavy, and now empty, ammo drum on the floor.

believing that was possible until this moment. Had they been alive, both would be unconscious or dead thanks to his attack. Now he knew better and needed to act fast, before more lives were lost.

Dropping a smoke pellet to the ground, a ten-foot area was suddenly engulfed in heavy, thick black smoke. Agent X charged into the house, considering his next form of attack. His favored weapon, the gas gun, would be useless against the undead. They didn't need to breathe!

X X X

"W..w…why…?" Benny Molnar rasped. He was kneeling at Murder Legendre's feet, dressed only in his underclothes. The mad mystic sat in Benny's desk chair, dressed in the expensive clothes the gangster wore earlier that night.

"Why? Why did I make you a zombie? I should think that would be obvious, my friend." Legendre replied with a snort. "I do not work for others. Murder Legendre is always the master."

Benny's head quivered as he tried to shake his head. "N..n…no. Why… m…m…my…p…p…plan?"

Murder Legendre straightened slightly, smiling as he comprehended the question. He rubbed his hands together with open delight. "Ah! I see your meaning now. You do not understand why I agreed to your rather peculiar idea for making you some sort of master of crime. Am I correct?"

Benny lowered his head slightly, unwilling to try and speak again. The evil sorcerer allowed him some weak control of his speech, delighting in the torment this brought to Benny Molnar. No cruelty appeared too minor for Murder Legendre's twisted tastes.

"That is quite simple. My new powers came with a price. My—patron, for lack of a better name, requires one simple payment. Chaos in the world. This mighty being with a thousand names has no desire for souls or paltry lives. He wishes fear and pain spread throughout the world. This I, Murder Legendre, promised him when we made our pact. In return, he gave to me the secret to deciphering the formulae of the book. Am I not spreading bedlam in the streets of this city? I think I shall do similar actions in every city. My powers only extend to five of my new type of zombies. I must now determine the number of my previous servants I may control." Murder Legendre mused and started to chuckle.

"B…b…but…" Benny tried to ask, but was cut off by a look from Legendre.

"Enough of your talk, my friend—my slave. The constant talk, talk, talk, from your mouth becomes tiresome. Your delusions are, while entertaining, ridiculous. Men in power would execute you before you uttered your first command. I may let them do so one day. For now, you stay in your current state for my amusement. Consider it a form of penance for forcing Murder Legendre to endure your foolish tongue." Legendre then turned his attention back to his books.

Benny Molnar silently wept as he knelt before the sorcerer, knowing shame and horror for the first time in his life.

X X X

Agent X dashed around a corner while reaching into his jacket pocket. He heard the staccato chatter of Mad Dog's Tommy gun. The insane undead killer was destroying anything in his path, his maniacal giggle just audible above the gunshots. The Big Man's guards were all away, either hiding or retreating to protect their leader in the upper floors.

X was unsure the best method of destroying dead man who not only walked, but fought back. This was not a true hindrance; there were many ways of confronting enemies. For one of the rare times in his career as a warrior against evil, he did not need to worry about the use of extreme force. He tried, if possible, to use his gas gun first and killed as a second choice.

Not today. These undead murderers were, somehow, walking about, talking and killing people. They did not appear able to die once again, but that was merely a challenge to Agent X. He possessed many tools in his war against crime, malicious cults, and evil espionage rings. Some were meant to be used to destroy machines or locks. They would serve as weapons against these two unkillable killers.

Pulling out a black ball about the size and shape of a child's marble, Agent X squeezed the outer shell until he felt a snap. He then counted to three and tossed the ball around the corner.

"Hey, there he is!" Legs Diamond shouted just before a low explosion rocked the area. Behind the wall, X covered his ears and felt the vibration of a high-intensity explosive.

These marbles were his own design, a mini-explosive that packed as much power as Mill's bomb. Dropping low X glanced around the corner, spotting Mad Dog and Legs. Their clothes were torn and tattered, but they were rising and reaching for their guns and hats.

"That rat tried to blow us up!" Mad Dog snarled, tilting his hat at the rakish angle he used as his signature look. The hat possessed two gaping holes and was stained charcoal with dust from the floor and walls of the mansion.

"He don't know that nothing can put down Jack Diamond. You get that, kid? Bring out all the guns and bombs you like! I don't die!" Legs Diamond shouted. He then spotted X and fired off a pair of shots. Both bullets missed as X ducked behind the wall and ran up the back stairs.

Pounding feet followed X as he ran up to the second level. Mad Dog's insane giggle floated through the air as they approached. Agent X reached to his back for a weapon he believed would end these two instantly. Then an idea struck him, a method of defeating this pair and whoever was responsible for their animation. X knew, from his reading of the turgid works of occult scholars, that a magus of great power was responsible for the undead gangsters. Either that or a scientist of uncanny malevolent vision. It didn't matter which, he needed to stop this abomination from occurring again.

Reaching into a pocket, Agent X pulled out another marble sized explosive. He broke the hard shell and tossed the charge down the stairs. The heavy explosion shook the house seconds later and he turned and ran up to the third floor. The explosive would not kill either Legs Diamond or Mad Dog Coll—but it would slow them down and give X a chance to act.

Near the landing on the third story, X lowered himself to the floor and peeked up the stairwell. A simple truism—people on guard rarely look high or low after a few minutes. This served Agent X well many times in the past. Hopefully it would again.

He was in luck, as he spotted a small knot of five men, all armed with shotguns. They stood in a tight knot with a heavy wooden door at their rear. Perfect, exactly what X needed to make his plan work.

Reaching under his arm, he pulled out his gas gun. Shifting a lever, and twisting a dial, he was now ready. Pointing the gun at the gangsters, he fired once, sending a heavy plume of gas their direction. He quickly ducked back as the yelps and explosions of shotgun rounds charged the air. Then the volley slacked off as the men dropped to the floor. X counted to five and stepped around the corner. The gangsters lay strewn about the corridor, their bodies slack and unmoving.

Glancing at the wooden door, Agent X was impressed by thickness of the wood as well as the impressive construction. A solid piece of wood with a heavy lock. It would take him twenty to thirty seconds to pick the lock, time he didn't have to waste. There was simply no time to be subtle.

Snatching up one of the fallen shotguns, X raised the heavy weapon and fired twice at the door. He wasn't aiming for the door or lock—shooting those areas was usually a slow, exacting process. No, he fired at a far more vulnerable area—the hinges. This was an old Chicago police trick, one Agent X used on rare occasions.

The door shook with the impact and, after a swift kick, he crashed into the room. Agent X was already at the side of the door when the retorts of revolver fire emerged from the room. Reaching up high, X fired his gas gun again and was greeted by a pair of gasps and the sounds of two falling bodies. Again he counted to five and stepped into the room.

The Big Man and O'Bannon lay slumped on the floor, their bodies unmoving. This gas, the strongest in X's arsenal was miraculous stuff. Made from certain plants he discovered in South and Central America, the victim was sedated so deeply, they appeared dead. They would, like the men in the hallway, remain in this state for up to five hours.

Pulling out a tube from his portable disguise kit, X covered the faces of the Big Man and O'Bannon. Now they were covered with a viscous crimson fluid that resembled blood. Both men looked like gangland homicide victims as they lay on the floor of the study.

Rubbing a little on his own face, Agent X lay upon the floor. His breathing slowed, his heartbeat grew fainter with each passing second. In less than a minute he no longer appeared to be breathing, there were no signs of life visible in his body. This was a skill Agent X learned while training in the mysterious East in his quest to be a secret agent without peer. This skill saved his life on many occasions; allowing him to appear void of life while remaining aware of all occurrences in his area.

Several minutes later he heard the voices of Coll and Diamond as they reached the third floor. "Hey! Look at this!" Diamond shouted.

Coll stepped up the landing and spied the fallen forms. He fired a spray of bullets above the bodies and another set near where they lay. "They're dead! Not a twitch out of them!"

"I heard shots, but I don't see any blood." Diamond stooped and checked a man's neck. No pulse or breathing were apparent. "Yeah, they're gone."

"Maybe they died of fright. You and me coming up after them gave them the willies so bad, they dropped like mackerels." Mad Dog mused and giggled. He stepped over the bodies; his gun raised, and entered the study.

The carnage was evident, three dead bodies, the Big Man among the bunch. Blood was all over their faces and bodies and none were moving.

"Yeah, dead here too." Legs Diamond stated and stiffened. Mad Dog Coll also straightened and they turned, their movements slower and less controlled. They lurched from the room, neither speaking or demonstrating any form of the life they had shown earlier.

X sat up and smiled, hearing their slow movement down the stairs. He reached for the Big Man's telephone. Dialing a familiar number, he spoke a quick series of passwords.

"Agent X?" K-9's gravelly voice asked. The sometimes controller of Secret Agent X never seemed to be away from his office.

"Yes. The gangster called the Big Man was attacked in his home; long story. He and all his men are dead or unconscious. Get your men down here and you can wrap up this whole gang. He'll be out cold for hours." With that, X cut the connection and ran from the room. He spotted Coll and Diamond as they were heading out the front door, their movements slow, jerky, and inhuman.

Following the pair was simplicity itself. They walked with a complete lack of awareness as to their surroundings. Tailing them was slow, but could be accomplished by a child. Thirty minutes later he walked a step behind them into the elevator at 55 Central Park West. There was no need to be subtle, not with these shambling undead creatures.

As the elevator doors opened. Agent X stepped into the penthouse. He pulled from beneath his arm a different gun. This one was a gift from an amazing man, a warrior against evil who was raised by a lost tribe in Africa. A genius, he gifted X with one of his favorite weapons after they worked in partnership one time.

"Who are you?" Murder Legendre asked as X stepped into the study a pace behind the zombified Mad Dog Coll and Legs Diamond.

"I was about to ask you the same question. Are you responsible for these abominations?" Agent X asked, raising his gun.

"I am." Legendre replied and folded his hands together slowly, placing the left thumb ceremonially on top of his fist. "It is no matter. I shall kill you and make you a lesser zombie. I require servants."

Just then, Legs Diamond and Mad Dog Coll straightened. They turned, their eyes aware, their faces creasing into smiles as they spotted X a few steps away.

"Well, well, well. Look who we have here! Our old pal. Looks like he was playing dead." Legs Diamond crooned.

Mad Dog Coll giggled and raised his Tommy Gun. "Time to stop playing games. Ready to die, buddy?"

Agent X didn't answer. Instead he fired the small gun in his hand at Coll watching with rapt attention as a volcanic hot stream of liquid and gas emerged from the barrel and engulfed the undead gangster. X fired a second time, consuming Legs Diamond with the thermogenic current. Both gangsters transformed into undead pyres in mere seconds, their ex-animated flesh unable to resist the molten blaze.

Murder Legendre backed away, but did not appear unduly concerned. The reason was apparent a moment later as he was joined by two more figures. Giuseppe "the Clutch Hand" Morello and Yee "Girlface" Toy. Morello snarled and raised his sawed-off shotgun.

"*Morire bastardo!*" Morello roared and pulled the trigger.

Agent X dove to the side, but still felt the sting as several pellets struck his right arm and chest. He winced in pain, but gripped his gun tighter. Firing, he hit Morello just as the man swiveled his shotgun. The dead gang leader opened his mouth to yell, but was instantly aflame.

Yee Toy snarled and leapt forward, his huge highbinder blade aiming for Agent X's throat. The incredible speed of the attack forced the agent to backpedal and raise his gun to block. The undead Tong killer was far too close to shoot, X himself would be incinerated by the unbelievable heat and flame.

The heavy steel blade bit deep into the flame gun's barrel and shattered. The incredibly dense metal was twisted by the impact, rendering the weapon useless. X tossed the weapon aside as Yee Toy reached into his jacket and pulled out a heavy revolver.

The Tong gangster raised the pistol and said, "*Si gwailo!*" which roughly translated to mean, "die ghostface". A common Tong battle cry when facing a Caucasian enemy.

X didn't reply, he stepped closer and grabbed Yee Toy's wrist with one hand and the gun with the other. With a wrench, the weapon was torn from the gangster's fist.

Yee Toy didn't waste time marveling at the precise disarming. His left foot swung out in a quick arc, slicing the back of X's hand. This forced the agent to open his hand involuntarily and send the handgun tumbling to the floor. He kicked the gun backwards, away from Yee Toy. Though a smart move defensively, it allowed the Tong killer a chance to hook punch to X's injured side. Yee Toy followed that with a knifehand strike to the neck, which Agent X blocked with a forearm.

X fired a knuckle strike to Yee Toy's throat, which missed when the latter ducked. The Tong killer fired three kick punches to Agent X's injured side, smiling as two struck home and caused a shot of agony up his side.

The Agent knew he could not stand and exchange strikes with this undead killer. Yee Toy was an expert with his hands, feet and weapons, an assassin feared by all of the underworld. This version would not feel the pain of X's attacks, only the living felt true pain. Agent X knew he needed to end this fast. An idea struck him as he blocked a kick from the gangster and drove him back with a hard punch to the jaw. Any living man would be senseless, feeling as if he was hit in the head by a mallet. Not Yee Toy. The undead killer merely shook his head and smiled, moving in again on the attack.

X waded in and absorbed a kick and a punch, wincing in pain. He pretended to stumble and step back, causing Yee Toy to sneer and step in for the kill. Exactly as Agent X predicted.

Pulling out his final marble bomb, X jammed the small object into Yee Toy's mouth. He then fired a vicious uppercut the jaw that shattered the casing and activated the explosive. With a harsh guttural roar, X kicked the undead Tong assassin in the chest, sending him tumbling backwards. As Yee Toy sailed back, the agent threw himself to the ground and covered his ears and head.

A heavy explosion rocked the penthouse and threw X several inches into the air. He stood a moment later, viewing the tattered remains of Yee Toy: alias Girlface. There was very little left to the man. While a human body can absorb an incredible amount of impact externally, internally is another matter entirely.

Opening the door X spotted Murder Legendre; he was surprised to see the man still present. A kneeling man in soiled undergarments slowly glanced his direction as the mustachioed magus gathered up a series of bottles in a bag. A massive leather-bound book was under his arm, held possessively and slowing his progress in packing.

"Benny," Murder Legendre stated, not looking up. "Kill this man for me now."

Benny Molnar rose up like a puppet on strings. Suddenly he was himself again, his mind and mouth his own. His body belonged to the Haitian sorcerer and he stepped towards Agent X. "Sorry, Mister. I don't want to obey him but I can't—"

X nodded and stood still, letting Benny approach. "I understand."

Benny's hands reached out, seeking X's throat. Just when he was about to grab the agent's neck, X grabbed both of the undead man's wrists. He then dropped back, bringing Benny's body along for the ride. Agent X's feet then rose and, as his back hit the floor, hurdled Benny Molnar over his head and sent him sailing out of the study window. The man who dreamed of being named the boss of bosses smiled as the window shattered and he flew out into empty space. As his body plummeted towards the Earth, he knew a merciful end was near.

Murder Legendre looked up at the sound of shattering glass, his eyes wide as Agent X climbed to his feet. Extending one claw like hand, he stated, "Stop!"

X found himself pressed back, as if an invisible hand was thrusting at his body. Sweat beaded his forehead as he took a slow step forward.

Legendre's eyes glowed and he snarled, "I order you, stop! I am your master!"

Agent X gritted his teeth so hard his jaw pulsed with pain. He took another slow step forward, feeling his mind weakening under the powerful mental assault of this man.

Smiling as he felt the contest swinging in his favor, Murder Legendre said, "You will stop. You cannot stand against my will."

Sensing the terrible magus was winning, X decided to take one final chance. Reaching a hand into his jacket, he pulled out a small flask. With his final effort of will, Agent X pushed off the stopper with a thumb and threw the vial at the book under Murder Legendre's arm. The glass did not shatter, but the liquid contents splattered across the book's cover. The magus howled in pain and dropped the weighty tome, his arm burned by the acid.

"The book! No!" Murder Legendre, seeing the acid eating through the cover and into the delicate pages inside. He dropped to his knees and screamed as his hands came into contact with the terrible chemical X carried in case of an emergency.

Agent X felt the pressing weight of the magus's mind leave his as the man screeched and tried to save his terrible tome. Realizing this monster was behind all the evil of the last few days, X realized he had no choice but to act. Raising his hand, he brought the knife edge down on Murder Legendre's skull, killing the man instantly. The terrible master of mystic evil fell to the side, lying next to his precious, soon to be destroyed book. The battle was over.

Agent X slumped against the desk, more exhausted and in pain than he had been in years. He reached for the phone to call K-9. This would be a difficult cleanup.

THE END

"Two worlds, not colliding"

Another Secret Agent X adventure, but this one was closer to my real loves than any I've written in the past. Don't get me wrong, Agent X is one of my truly favorite heroes; a character that was one of the first pulp legends I've ever read. But my true love—one since I was little—appeared in this tale.

Horror; the original black and white films that were old when I was a child watching them on flickering library projectors or a black and white television in my parent's basement. I was blessed as a kid with a pair of parents who were film lovers—both of whom were determined to share their knowledge with me as I grew up. I was four or five when I first watched the great giant monster movies; the original KING KONG as well as several of the GODZILLA series. I was hooked, which also meant I could be kept quiet for a few hours every time one of these films appeared on the screen. This must have been a good respite for my mom and dad, I was a hyperactive little bundle of noise.

It was when I was six that I really learned about great horror. It was Spring Break at school and our local library decided to offer a free film festival for kids every day for a week. Their subject matter? The original Universal monster series. Over a week I viewed Dracula, the Frankenstein Monster, the Wolfman, and the Mummy—all in chronological order—while lying on a hard wood floor. Can you imagine it? These days the library would probably be hip deep in lawsuits over the subject matter alone.

Still, the actors and their characters were so familiar, none quite so much as Bela Lugosi. There was just something powerfully commanding about the way he carried himself, the way he spoke every line with that deep, dramatic delivery. I was a fan and even checked out a book on monster movies that week. I'm fairly certain all I did was look at the pictures, but the seed was sown.

Around the same period, I stumbled onto Bela's most chilling performance as the evil Voodoo Sorcerer "Murder" Legendre in the low-budget masterpiece, WHITE ZOMBIE. This film, a public domain classic, has Bela enslaving and destroying men and women with a sadistic glee that I still consider one of the greatest portrayals of supernatural evil in cinema. Every line he uttered, every time he laughed his mocking, demonic laugh, I was unable to move. I still feel that way when he intones the line about his zombies, "For you, my friend, they are the angels of death."

Few actors could pull off such a line, but the great Bela pulled it off with delight. Sadly, these days he's mostly known for the sadness of his later life—his fall into addiction. I prefer him as the larger-than-life "Murder" Legendre, the Satanist with some decency Dr. Vitus Werdegast in THE BLACK CAT, and of course, Dracula. The last, of course, is his best-known role and influential in ways we can't begin to comprehend to this day.

Therefore I consider this story one of my most satisfying pulp writing experiences, bringing these two favorite worlds of mine together. Who knows if I'll ever get a chance to do it again. Here's hoping.

X X X

FRANK SCHILDINER—is a martial arts instructor at Amorosi's Mixed Martial Arts in New Jersey. He is the writer of the novels THE QUEST OF FRANKENSTEIN, THE TRIUMPH OF FRANKENSTEIN and NAPOLEON'S VAMPIRE HUNTERS. Frank is a regular contributor to the fictional series TALES OF THE SHADOWMEN and has been published in THE NEW ADVENTURES OF THUNDER JIM WADE; SECRET AGENT X Volumes 3, 4, 5; and THE AVENGER: THE JUSTICE FILES. He resides in New Jersey with his wife Gail, who is his top supporter, and two cats who are indifferent on the subject.

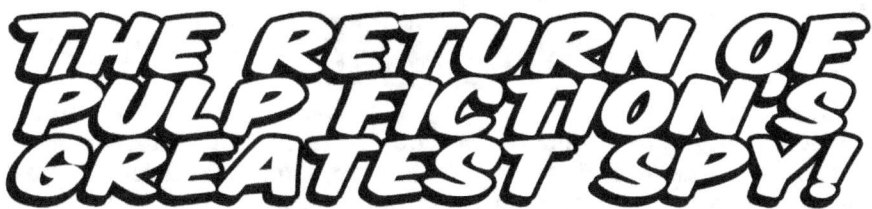

THE RETURN OF PULP FICTION'S GREATEST SPY!

Secret Agent X, the original super-spy, is back in these five stellar collections. Written by today's best New Pulp Writers, the Man of a Thousand Faces once again defends America from all manner of evil threats.

Arguably the most popular character at Airship 27, here are the first five exciting installments in the Anthology series. Welcome to the daring exploits of pulpdom's original super-spy as brought to you by Airship 27 Productions!

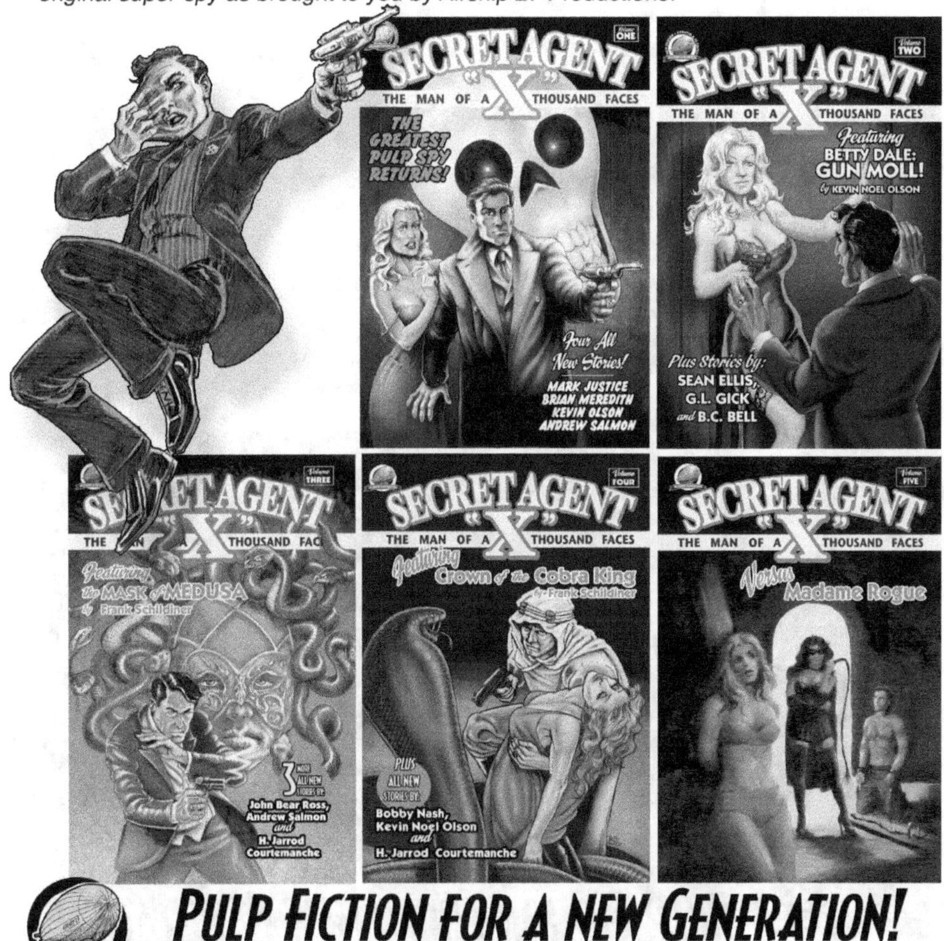

AN AIRSHIP 27 PRODUCTION

PULP FICTION FOR A NEW GENERATION!

AVAILABLE AT AMAZON.COM, BOOKSTORES WORLDWIDE AND AS A PDF EBOOK AT AIRSHIP27HANGAR.COM

www.ingramcontent.com/pod-product-compliance
Lightning Source LLC
Chambersburg PA
CBHW051132260626
47170CB00005B/1771